ACT
OF FAITH

Also by Michael Bowen

Can't Miss
Badger Game
Washington Deceased
Fielder's Choice
Faithfully Executed

ACT
OF FAITH

MICHAEL
BOWEN

ST. MARTIN'S PRESS
NEW YORK

Act of Faith is a work of fiction. Except for well-known public figures referred to in passing, the characters depicted in the story do not exist and never have existed, and the events described did not take place. They are products of the author's imagination. Any resemblance between characters in the story and actual persons, living or dead, or between incidents in the narrative and actual occurrences, is purely coincidental and is not intended.

Grateful acknowledgment is made for permission to reprint "MLF Lullaby" copyright © 1964 by Tom Lehrer. Copyright renewed.

Design by Dawn Niles

Library of Congress Cataloging-in-Publication Data

Bowen, Michael.
    Act of faith : a Thomas and Sandrine Curry mystery / Michael Bowen.
    p. cm.
    ISBN 0-312-08694-6
    I. Title.
    PS3552.0864A28   1993
    813'.54—dc20   92-34424
                                                   CIP

10 9 8 7 6 5 4 3 2 1

For Daniel Patrick Bowen, D.V.M.

"A ship in harbor is safe,
but that is not the
purpose of a ship."
—John Shedd

Gallia est omnis divisa in partes tres, quarum unam incolunt Belgae,
aliam Aquitani, tertiam qui ipsorum lingua Celtae, nostra Galli appellan-
tur. . . . Horum omnium fortissimi sunt Belgae. . . .

[All Gaul is divided into three parts, inhabited respectively by
the Belgians, the Aquitanians, and those who call themselves Celts
and whom we know as Gauls. . . . Of all these, the Belgians are the
bravest. . . .]

—Julius Caesar, *Commentaries on the Gallic Wars* (52 B.C.)

I say a bygone should be a bygone.
Let's make peace
The way we did
In Stanleyville and Saigon.

—Tom Lehrer, "MLF Lullaby" (1964)

Muramvya Inn
Floor Plan

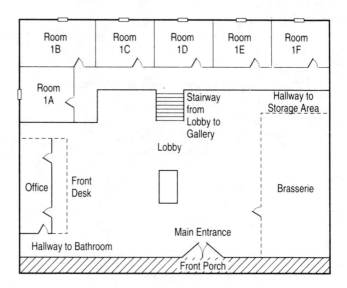

Room 1B

Room 1C

Room 1D

Room 1E

Room 1F

Room 1A

Stairway from Lobby to Gallery

Hallway to Storage Area

Lobby

Office

Front Desk

Brasserie

Main Entrance

Hallway to Bathroom

Front Porch

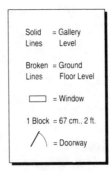

Solid Lines = Gallery Level

Broken Lines = Ground Floor Level

▭ = Window

1 Block = 67 cm., 2 ft.

⌒ = Doorway

Prologue

On July 6, 1963, Michel Ndala asked Claude Devereaux to kill Alex Hanson. Ndala was holding a copy of Devereaux's death warrant at the time. Under the circumstances, Devereaux said yes.

The fact that Thomas and Sandrine Curry were at that moment less than fifty miles away was *not* my fault. I'm rather sensitive on the point, so let's get it straight right away. I was in Leopoldville trying to bring a French client, a Congolese government construction contract, and a U.S. foreign-aid grant into simultaneous contact.

It's true that I'd asked Sandy to come with me. My French was fluent but hers was perfect, and I figured that might come in handy.

It's also true that I expected Thomas to tag along so they could squeeze a vacation out of it. And I suppose I must've realized that something sane, like hopping over to Kenya so they could hit a couple of game parks and sip gin and tonics on the veranda of the Nairobi Hilton, wasn't exactly their style. But no law said they had to spend their holiday gallivanting around the back end of nowhere in Burundi during one of the very few months in human history when events in central Africa actually engaged the attention of the white world.

Thomas pulled me into the thing toward the end, so I picked up that part on my own. It took me quite a while to get the rest of the story straight, especially during the many years when Thomas and Sandy were uncharacteristically reticent about it. I might've taken the hint and let it drop, except for that sensitive point I mentioned. Anyhow, here's the way it happened.

1

The cross hairs intersected about five centimeters below the bull elephant's left eye. Scarcely trusting herself to breathe, lying as flat as she could on the African plain, Sandy tightened her index finger on the trigger.

"You can shoot now," Laurent Dray said.

Frowning with concentration, Sandy took a breath and let half of it out. She squeezed the trigger.

"Got it," she muttered as the Pentax's shutter snapped.

"Excellent," Thomas said. "Let's take nine or ten dozen more before we get back on the horses." Thomas's approach to horseback riding was more earnest than enthusiastic.

An easy smile replaced Sandy's intense grimace. Rolling to a sitting position, she disconnected the cable release and unscrewed the pistol grip from the bottom of the three-hundred-millimeter telephoto lens on the camera.

Thomas pulled an olive drab duffel bag over to his wife. Dray watched with bemused patience as the young woman methodically detached the lens, capped it at either end, stowed it in the bag in a padded leather case, replaced it on the camera body with a standard lens, and draped the camera by a strap from her shoulder.

"This is the first photographic outing I have guided in years," Dray said as Thomas and Sandy moved toward their horses. Adjusting his bush hat, his white teeth especially brilliant in his deeply tanned face, Dray climbed into a clean but battered British Landrover topped with an improvised canvas roof. "What most of my clients shoot with is measured in calibers rather than millimeters."

"The big kills," Thomas nodded. He swung with less than unmitigated relish into the saddle of his horse.

"Exact," Dray said. "French, Belgian, British, American, makes no difference. They are all after trophy game."

Sandy hoisted the duffel bag into the back of the Landrover. She took an extra minute to make sure that the restraining straps properly secured it.

"We prefer our large game alive," she commented. "I think it was an American who said that if you destroy something men made you are called a vandal, but if you destroy something God made you are called a sportsman."

"You disdain recreational hunting, madame?" Dray gibed playfully. "I view it simply as a sport like any other."

"A distinctly minor sport," Thomas said. "Not unlike horseback riding in that respect."

" 'Minor.' " Dray paused, his face a picture of thoughtful contemplation, as if he were giving the proposition grave consideration. "But Monsieur Curry, can one truly draw a principled and rigorous distinction between what you call minor sports and the other variety?"

"Certainly," Thomas said. "A minor sport is one that I wouldn't watch on television unless there were Communists on the other side."

"Both principled and rigorous, you must agree," Sandy said.

"But not altogether serious, I suspect," Dray smiled. "Whereas your objection, Madame Curry, if I am not mistaken, reflects a more substantive attitude."

"You are correct. I dislike hunting on the merits. I cannot imagine discovering pleasure in taking an animal's life purely

4

for the sake of killing it—and if I did find pleasure in it I would be disappointed in myself for doing so."

"Many of my clients would be tempted to ask if you are therefore a vegetarian as well."

"Certainly not," Sandy answered quickly as she mounted her horse. "I disapprove of killing animals as an end in itself. I have no objection to doing so as a necessary means to an independently desirable objective."

"A first-rate meal qualifies as an independently desirable objective, in case you were wondering," Thomas interjected. "As Sartre recently pointed out."

"Are you entirely sure it was Sartre?" Sandy asked, smiling innocently. "It sounds remarkably levelheaded for him."

"Perhaps it was Jerry Lewis," Thomas conceded. "Someone, at any rate, whose genius *le Tout Paris* has recently certified."

"Your views on hunting are intriguing in a soldier's daughter," Dray said to Sandy. "Wars are often fought for reasons far less noble than pleasure. Why is it blameworthy to kill animals for sport but morally defensible to kill men in war?"

"Because animals very seldom have it coming," Sandy answered. This time she wasn't smiling.

"This is a topic on which we are not going to agree," Dray said with warm, unruffled humor. "So I will conclude our discussion with the sturdy American bromide that the customer is always right. If we move with dispatch, there should still be two hours of light left when we reach the campsite."

The heavily laden Landrover coughed into life and began lurching across the countryside at about eight miles an hour, while Thomas and Sandy coaxed their horses along behind its brand new, nine-digit, green-on-red KINGDOM OF BURUNDI license plate.

Dray told me later that he was particularly encouraged by the fact that in the thirty hours he'd been guiding Thomas and Sandy around the Burundi backcountry, he hadn't heard them exchange a single harsh word or cutting remark. He was certain that their apparently carefree enjoyment of each other's company couldn't survive such perfect manners much longer. Sedulous politeness in a married couple, in his experience, infallibly presaged an impending blowup. He planned to be in easy hailing distance of Sandy when the fireworks started.

The inchoate tension between Thomas and Sandy that Dray thought he sensed might be explained easily enough. Sandy was quintessentially French, from the tips of her feet to her royal blue Norman eyes, staring customarily with disarming directness out of a face that otherwise evoked the Midi with Mediterranean eloquence. Her favorite sport was fencing. Her favorite opera was *Carmen*. Her favorite food was any meat or fish with a properly made sauce, and her favorite drink was champagne.

Sandy had spent much of her childhood in French colonial Africa, for which her father only eight years before had died in an unnamed battle of a soon-to-be-forgotten war. Sandy would have died with him if a nationalist gunrunner named Thomas Curry hadn't been available with a helicopter and an acute desire to save his own skin. How she got from Algeria to New York where she picked up a girl-Friday job from me and a ring from Thomas is another story.

I'm Theodore Furst, by the way. International lawyer, partner of Thomas's father, T. Graham Curry. T. Graham does criminal law. How can a small, specialized firm fit criminal law and international law together into a sensible working arrangement? Think about it.

So, anyway, here was Sandy in freshly independent Burundi next door to the Congo, where in 1963 the European colonial adventure was being buried with something short of full military honors. The United States wasn't exactly dancing on the grave, but a sensitive European might have been forgiven for thinking that we were holding the coats of people who were. Confronting a past that the world had now repudiated, accompanied by the man for whom she herself had turned her back on it, you'd expect a little tension, wouldn't you?

Well, that shows what you know. Sandy was made of tougher stuff than that. So was Thomas, although people often didn't find out until it was too late. Neither of them was cut out for angst-ridden nombril gazing. What Dray's sensitive antennae were picking up was a bit simpler and a bit more serious at the same time.

Thomas and Sandy had come of age in a world at war, spiritually desolate and riven by blood and terror. The twentieth century's implacable appetite for violent death had torn them both. Sandy had lost a father to nationalist machine guns in Algeria. Thomas had lost a mother to Maoist artillery in Nanking. They were young, healthy, and hungry for life. They had been married for a little over a year. Despite assiduous effort, they hadn't yet conceived a child. And, without being able to come out and say it or perhaps even admit it to themselves, they couldn't help beginning to wonder why.

The small party stopped a little over an hour later on a stretch of level ground between a gently sloping hill and a churning brown stream. Dray built a fire while Thomas and Sandy unloaded the Landrover and labored to put up their old-fashioned, heavy canvas tent.

Dray seemed to spend more time with the fire than fires usually took. When he'd finally finished, he unzipped the cover on the spare tire mounted on the back of the Landrover, took a small cardboard box from the tire's well, then moved to the right rear of the vehicle and squatted beside the tire there. Drawing a strip of patching rubber out of the box, he smeared it with some goop from a tube in the box, heated it for a few seconds with his lighter, and pressed the patch onto a shiny place just below the tread welt.

He's stalling, Thomas thought as he watched the elaborate process.

"I have developed some misgivings about the arrangements we originally discussed," Dray said over his shoulder as he finished. "I have never left a group I was guiding alone overnight before."

"You gave us fair warning," Thomas said. "We called you on short notice with improvised plans. You said you had something else to attend to tonight and tomorrow. We discussed it and decided that was no problem. Don't give it another thought."

"That discussion took place in Bujumbura, whereas we are confronting the actual situation in the bush," Dray said. Turning around as he stood, he folded his arms across his chest and leaned against the Landrover. "In Bujumbura the

7

Congo seemed like a theoretical problem. Here it seems like a very real one.''

"I thought the UN peacekeeping force has had things under control in the Congo for several months," Thomas said. "That was the story in Leopoldville."

"Supposedly," Dray conceded grudgingly. "I happen to know there are still some rebels running around Katanga Province, whether Leopoldville admits it or not."

"Perhaps so," Thomas said. "But Katanga's a long way from here, and the border between us and the Congo's supposed to be secure. That's why we came to Burundi instead of staying in the Congo for our vacation in the first place. The U.S. Embassy said that Burundi was quiet."

" 'Quiet' does not mean inactive," Dray countered with an uneasy smile. "The rebels behave while they are in Burundi because they use it as a sanctuary. But you can be certain they are here from time to time."

"Still," Sandy said, "you told us this site was less than two kilometers from a border guardpost. Even if the Katangans do plan on a border-crossing, they should choose a spot farther away. I think we will be all right."

Dray looked unconvinced. Thomas and Sandy shrugged at each other.

"Well," Dray said decisively. "Good luck. I will see you here tomorrow night."

He slid behind the wheel and drove off.

Thomas slipped behind his wife and crossed his arms under her breasts. Leaning against him, Sandy offered Thomas a contented smile as she watched Dray drive off. Any incipient tension they may have felt receded as the Landrover pulled away.

"It was very naughty of you to make that remark about Sartre and Jerry Lewis," she said. "People like Dray think all Americans are earnest. It disorients them to encounter one like you."

"View it as a necessary means to an independently desirable objective," Thomas said.

"You are wicked," Sandy said, playfully slapping his hand.

That they didn't use the last hour or so of daylight to take

8

more pictures is purely surmise on my part. That they enjoyed a blissful evening alone together is also surmise. My surmises are accurate as a general rule—and I really hope these two are, because a lot of things were going to change before the next blissful evening they'd enjoy that way.

2

From the top of a hill not quite half a mile from their campsite, Sandy watched the next morning's sunrise. It started delicately, as a scarcely perceptible change in the quality of the light reflecting from the clouds lying low in the east. A soft pink layering of the cloud bank followed. Then, all at once, about three degrees above the horizon, the burnt orange disk appeared fully formed, seeming to promise an ascent to midsky before her eyes.

Kneeling at the base of a tripod, Sandy used her cable release to hold the Pentax's shutter open for ten seconds. After advancing the film, she held it open for twenty seconds. Then she shot a thirty-second time exposure.

"Tea?" Thomas asked when she'd finished the third one.

"Yes, thank you." She turned and accepted a canteen full of warm Earl Grey. "I did not hear you come up."

"I could tell you were concentrating."

"Dray is an interesting type, wouldn't you say?" Sandy asked after a generous swallow.

"Fascinating," Thomas agreed. "Knows his way around,

10

competent, careful. Has that indecipherable disregard for self-importance that Belgians are so famous for. Plus, he does something Americans find particularly charming in French-speakers."

"And what is that?" Sandy demanded with a wary smile.

"When an American talks to him in French, he answers in French."

"*Ne boudes pas,*" Sandy teased.

"*Parles plus lentement, s'il te plait. Je ne parle pas français très bien.*"

"Excuse me?" Sandy asked innocently.

"Mrs. Curry, you are being deliberately provocative."

"I understand that is something Americans find particularly charming in the French."

"Keep it up. I might just take you up on it."

Sandy handed him the canteen and began replacing the standard lens on the Pentax with a telephoto.

"Take me up on it after I photograph that convoy in the distance."

Thomas gazed through the dissipating morning haze at a short procession of vehicles winding sinuously across pale green and dark brown countryside half a mile or so away. It was easy to see why she wanted the picture. An open-bed, ten-ton stake truck piled high with bulging burlap bags was followed by a light blue school bus. An aging Renault sedan crawled behind the bus, with what looked to Thomas like a burlap-stuffed hay wagon bringing up the rear. Framed by the rainwashed African scenery, the incongruous assemblage might have come straight out of *National Geographic*.

"Intriguing mix," he muttered. "They—"

"Thomas, look at this," Sandy interrupted, her voice quietly urgent.

Jerking his head around, Thomas saw Sandy abandon the camera and begin looking hastily around the hilltop. He scurried to the tripod.

"Where is the canteen?" she demanded.

"There." He pointed to the ground at his right as he squinted through the viewfinder. "Why?"

The moment he had the question out he knew the answer. Through the telephoto lens he spotted four men in dark green camouflage uniforms lying tensely in tall grass twenty feet from the road. At least two of them had rifles. The lead truck was no more than twenty yards from the site of the impending ambush.

How many more ambushers he might have spotted if he'd panned the camera was something Thomas never learned. Even as he raised his right hand to the tripod handle, a dark gray cloud burst violently from underneath the big truck's rear wheels. In eerie silence the truck leaped sideways on the dirt-and-gravel roadway while the school bus braked furiously, crumpling its nose on the truck's chassis. The Renault stopped without hitting the bus, but the hay-wagon truck rear ended it. Only half a second later did the noise of an explosive thump and grinding crash reach them.

Over his right shoulder, something drew Thomas's eye. Sandy had pulled the cover from their canteen and was swinging the shiny body in exaggerated arcs over her head. It was pure reflex, a desperate attempt to warn the helpless vehicles of the danger they'd been approaching, hopelessly late the instant her effort started.

"Sandy!" Thomas yelled.

He leaped at her from his crouch behind the camera, catching her around the waist with his left arm in an artless playground tackle. He grunted as he slammed to the ground with his wife.

"What do you think you are doing?" she demanded hotly.

"Remembering General Porter's last words: 'They couldn't hit an elephant at this dist—' "

"Absurd," she snapped. "They are a kilometer away. I was in no danger whatever."

In elegant rebuttal the telephoto lens abruptly shattered as the tripod flipped backward. They heard splintered glass tinkling at the same instant as the report of the shot that had hit the camera came to them.

"I stand corrected," Sandy admitted with grim wonder.

They lay in numb silence for a moment, unable to pull their eyes from the orange muzzle flashes spattering in the distance.

"We can lie here and watch a massacre," Thomas said, "or we can haul ourselves out of here."

"If they are on foot," Sandy said, "we can easily outdistance them on the horses. If they have vehicles, it will make no difference whether we run now or in five minutes. There might be something we can do if we stay."

"Fair enough," Thomas agreed.

The expected massacre, however, failed to develop. The ambushers peppered the stricken convoy with gunfire, but they didn't move in on it. Disciplined bursts of automatic weapons fire from inside the bus and beneath the hay-wagon truck explained their reticence. No panicky, full-clip, lead spraying. Two- and three-shot blasts at picked targets.

"There are some soldiers down there who know what they're doing," Thomas said.

"Thank God," Sandy replied.

The standoff had continued for less than three minutes when Thomas and Sandy pricked up their ears at a sound they'd both heard before: the twentieth-century equivalent of a cavalry bugler blowing *Charge!*—a whining, whuppa-whuppa-whuppa of four helicopter gunships.

With breathtaking suddenness the battle ended moments after the copters swung into sight and swooped explosively toward the fighting. Their universe instantly transformed into a smoky, flame-streaked hell of rockets and rattling .50-caliber machine guns, the ambushers broke and ran. Two of the helicopters landed near the road while the other two pursued the broken attackers, all but invisible now in billowing black smoke that enveloped the battlefield.

Among the soldiers who spilled from the landed helicopters, three detached themselves and began double-timing it toward the hill where Thomas and Sandy waited.

"All things considered," Thomas said, "I recommend that we sit tight."

"*D'accord,*" Sandy said.

She moved unhurriedly to the ruined camera and began removing the film from it. Curiously, it was only three eventful days later that Thomas began to wonder why.

3

Coffee, Thomas thought. Freshly harvested robusta coffee beans spilling from the two trucks and the perforated side of the school bus covered the roadside. A rich odor from cook fires suffused Thomas and Sandy and the soldiers with them when they were still two hundred yards away.

The small knapsack in which Thomas had salvaged a flashlight, some canned food, and a few other odds and ends rustled with crisp Kingdom of Burundi receipts: for their rifle, their horses, their tent, and miscellaneous camping equipment. And for the camera. The young, black, six-foot-eight-inch lieutenant had been very clear in demanding that, addressing the issue unambiguously in courteous, insistent French.

The crowd near the site of the attack was divided into two groups: people standing around and soldiers. Sandy watched troops still fanning out through the area where the ambushers had fled, loading lumpy, green body bags onto helicopters, tending the fires, cleaning rifles, and critically examining copter engines. The dozen or so survivors from the convoy stood or slouched or squatted in a static, uncertain semicircle in between the damaged vehicles and the first two helicopters. Two of them caught Sandy's attention. The first was a tall, massive black man wearing a navy blue suit, white shirt, solid blue tie, and, running diagonally across his barrel chest under his suit coat, a green, white, and red-striped silk sash. The other man Sandy noticed was white, a bit shorter than Thomas, medium framed, dressed in a khaki outfit that fell somewhere in between casual and military, like a tourist who'd outfitted himself with wardrobe remnants from *Lives of a Bengal Lancer.*

A revving copter engine precluded any immediate commentary on these observations. The farther helicopter lifted delicately off the ground and climbed toward the north. A major, who had crouched to avoid the prop-wash as the helicopter took off, straightened and strode toward them. He and the lieutenant exchanged clipped comments in what Thomas assumed to be Kirundi. The lieutenant handed Thomas's and Sandy's passports to the major, who examined them critically.

"I am Major Michel Ndala," he said to Thomas and Sandy then. He spoke in slow, carefully enunciated French, glancing speculatively from Thomas to Sandy as he did so. "According to these, you are American tourists on safari. Who was your guide?"

"Laurent Dray," Sandy said.

"Where is Monsieur Dray?"

"He said he had some matters to attend to. He took his Landrover yesterday afternoon and was expected to return tonight."

Ndala frowned. After tapping the passports for a moment on a long, bony thumb, he tendered them back to Thomas and Sandy.

"My apologies for this disruption of your plans," he said. "Under the circumstances, however, we must deem the environs too insecure for tourism. You will be taken with the others to Muramvya, the market town the convoy was headed for. There you will be put up until transport can be arranged to Bujumbura."

"When do you think that will be?" Sandy asked.

"Tomorrow at the latest," Ndala answered.

After receiving Sandy's thanks, he hustled away with Thomas and Sandy's erstwhile military escort in his wake.

"We're headed for someplace called Muramvya?" Thomas asked Sandy, to be sure he'd gotten the substance of the exchange right.

"Yes."

"When do we leave?"

"When they get around to taking us—and they do not seem to be in any particular hurry."

"Excuse me." They looked up at the French-accented English words. The sashed black man stood nearby, several inches over Thomas's six feet. "My name is Antoine Mboya. I am the principal *juge d'instruction* for the central judicial and administrative district of Burundi. You seem to have stumbled into our misadventure."

"That's exactly what we did," Thomas said. He introduced himself and Sandy. "Fortunately, it came out much better than it looked like it was going to."

"We were very lucky," Mboya said, nodding. "Soldiers with the convoy, a truck leading the way to take the brunt of the explosion, a coffee cargo on the bus that absorbed much of the terrorists' fire, attackers who lost their stomach for the fight rather quickly. I understand that we have only three missing from the convoy. It could easily have been much worse."

Mboya rattled off the names of four of the other survivors, standing a few feet away. The other seven—all black men shorter than Sandy—he didn't bother to name.

Three of the four he did identify were black, tall as he was, with long, full noses and smooth faces like his. Two of them were coffee growers and the third a bureaucrat according to Mboya's brief descriptions. The fourth was the white man in khaki. Mboya said that his name was Claude Devereaux.

"*Bonjour,*" Devereaux said, nodding briefly in their direction at the sound of his name.

"What is Monsieur Devereaux's field?" Sandy asked Mboya after she and Thomas had returned the perfunctory greeting. Devereaux glanced up again.

"*Génie,*" he responded before Mboya could, using a

16

French word that might mean either "engineering" or "genius."

"*Quelle sorte de génie êtes-vous?*" Thomas asked in junior-year-abroad French.

"The kind that survives," Devereaux answered in English. "I live on my income, *comme on dit.*"

Mboya laughed lightly. Then his eyes darted away from Thomas and Sandy.

"Excuse me, Major," he said as Ndala passed back within earshot. "Have you any idea when the ferrying to Muramvya will begin?"

"No, regretfully," Ndala said. He walked back over toward the group. "My apologies once again, Madame Curry. I was wondering whether by chance there was film in the camera you turned over to my men?"

"No," Sandy answered. "I took it out after the camera was ruined by the gunshot."

"May I have it, please?" It was an order, not a request. "There may be something on it that could help us prevent attacks like this in the future."

"Certainly," Sandy said. Rummaging through a pocket in her trousers she came up with a small, silver, screw-top canister and handed it to the soldier.

"Thank you," Ndala said. Then, to the lieutenant, "Write her a receipt."

Lunch highlighted the more than five hours that passed before the small group of civilians finally started boarding helicopters for the promised flight to Muramvya. Lunch in this case meant the Belgian armed forces equivalent of K-rations, which should give you an idea of what the rest of the wait was like. Thomas chose two oblong packets marked OEUFS/JAMBON. Thomas had served in Korea, and the superiority of breakfast selections over other offerings in the K-ration line was proverbial among American veterans of the era.

"What's a *juge d'instruction?*" Thomas asked Sandy quietly as they nibbled from the congealed, yellow-and-pink mass on the mess plate in front of them.

"The term does not lend itself to ready translation,"

17

Sandy said. "Literally, it means 'investigating magistrate.' But that does not truly capture what a *juge d'instruction* does."

"Which is what?"

"In Anglo-Saxon terms, he combines the functions of senior detective, prosecuting attorney, and preliminary-hearing judge. He has to investigate crimes, but he must also be rigorously independent of the police. He must present the evidence against an accused in court, but he must first make his own judgment about that person's guilt."

"Like a DA in New York," Thomas said.

"Not entirely. American district attorneys do not deliberately prosecute innocent people, but they are essentially advocates. The main thing they have to decide is whether they can *prove* guilt. If they become overzealous, a person falsely accused has a judge and a jury to appeal to."

"Not so with guys like Mboya?" Thomas asked skeptically.

"No. Once a *juge d'instruction* decides that an accused is guilty, the trial is likely to be a formality. In an inquisitorial system like most European colonies have inherited, it is much more important to have good investigating magistrates than to have good judges. If the *juge d'instruction* is corrupt or lazy or too close to the police, justice is impossible."

"In that case," Thomas said with dispassionate calm, "I hope Mboya's good. Because I think he's interested in us."

"One can hardly blame him," Sandy said. "He came upon two whites claiming to be tourists but wandering around without a guide a kilometer away from a terrorist attack."

"There is that," Thomas admitted.

"I think that younger man whom Mboya introduced as a *fonctionnaire* is actually his assistant," Sandy continued. "Mboya told him discreetly to radio Bujumbura and have someone contact the French and U.S. embassies for information about us."

"Somehow," Thomas said, "I'll be surprised if all of it is flattering."

The Muramvya expedition finally got under way about an hour after the meal. The two copters carrying the group landed a little after 1 P.M. in the teeming market town's central square, down the principal street from its church, a few dozen feet from its only inn. Flies buzzed in front of open-air shops. The distinctive odor of cooking vegetables washed over the square. Hordes of black children, the boys' hair cropped so close to their heads that from a distance they looked bald, scurried to the vicinity of the helicopters and then hung shyly back as people began to climb out of them.

While sergeants barked orders and short black men and boys in civvies unloaded luggage and carried it into the inn's lobby, Ndala led the survivors to an adjoining ground-floor brasserie. He summoned the inn's manager into the area, pored over a clipboard with him for a few minutes, then pounded twice on the bar to get the assembled group's attention.

"Unfortunately," he said in French, "the inn has only six guest rooms, all on the gallery level overlooking the lobby. I must appropriate Room 1A as my command post until we have satisfied ourselves that the surrounding area has been cleared of guerrilla activity. Monsieur Devereaux will share Room 1B with the guest already there."

"Excuse me, Major," Mboya said, leaping instantly at this comment. He flashed leather-bound credentials at Ndala and the inn manager. "Who is the guest already registered to Room 1B?"

"Terence Donoghue," the manager stammered as Ndala scowled impatiently.

"Nationality?" Mboya demanded.

"Irish."

"Is he the only foreign guest registered here?"

"At the moment."

"Where is his passport?"

"In our safe, of course," the manager said.

"You will if you please produce it for me as soon as the major is through with you."

"Very well."

From the inside pocket of his coat, Mboya produced a five-by-seven inch photograph.

"Do you recognize the person in this picture?"

The manager gave the picture a perfunctory glance.

"Hard to say," he answered with a leave-me-out-of-it shrug. "All whites look alike to me."

19

"As soon as possible, you will if you please show Monsieur Donoghue this picture and ask if he recognizes the person in it."

"Very well."

"May I continue?" Ndala asked acidly.

"By all means," Mboya said, his voice unruffled. "My apologies for the interruption."

"Rooms 1C and 1D will be allocated to the other officers with the contingent," Ndala resumed then. His clipped tones cut off the last syllable of Mboya's response. "And Room 1E will be shared by the NCOs. Room 1F will be assigned to Magistrate Mboya. We will set up camp-beds in this area for the rest of you. Understood?"

Nothing about the sleeping assignments struck Thomas as unexpected. Soldiers taken care of first and foremost, a senior Burundi civilian official provided with his own quarters, a European permanent resident allowed to share a private room, and everybody else shunted into an improvised dormitory. Thomas was surprised when Mboya spoke up.

"Excuse me again, if you please, Major," he said.

"Yes?"

"I very much appreciate your consideration. However, two of our companions in misfortune are husband and wife visiting this country. I would be happy to take a cot down here for the night so that they might have a room to themselves."

"Out of the question," Ndala snapped. "We must assume you are a target of any terrorists in the vicinity. We have gone to some trouble to get you to a secure area, and it would be derelict not to provide you with the maximum possible protection while you are here."

"Thanks for trying," Thomas said to Mboya.

Ndala nodded to a sergeant, who turned to a troop of the shorter Burundians standing in the doorway between the brasserie and the lobby. The sergeant clapped his hands and bellowed a couple of brisk commands at the group. The men immediately turned to gather military and civilian baggage and distribute it. The civilians shuffled through sawdust on the sandalwood floor, leaned against the zinc bar, looked at the motes floating in the afternoon sunlight, and confronted the prospect of spending the next twenty-four hours or so in

Muramvya without coffee to market, game to hunt, or cameras to play with.

"Why do the short chaps get all the dirty work?" Thomas whispered to Sandy.

"It is probably something tribal, but I am not certain," Sandy said. "Burundi was never a French colony. It was part of German East Africa and then was mandated to Belgium after World War I."

"If you want to see what France can do with a colony," Devereaux interjected in a low, patronizing voice, "go to Brazzaville or Bamako."

"Or Dien Bien Phu," Thomas offered, smiling but with a trace of irritation. Devereaux ignored him.

"So," Sandy said to Devereaux, "does that mean it is the Belgians' fault that the short ones get all the dirty work?"

"The tall ones are Watusi," Devereaux said. "They run things here, now that the Belgians have decamped. About one in every ten Burundians is Watusi. The short ones are Hutus. They're most of the other 90 percent. They get run." Devereaux glanced up at Thomas. "That's why the sergeant grins in your direction every time he tells the Hutus to do some heavy lifting."

"What do you mean?" Thomas asked.

"He's basking in your presumed American approval. He's saying, 'See, we treat our niggers the same way you treat yours.' "

Now, I know exactly what you're thinking: Isn't it a funny coincidence that Thomas, Sandy, and I just happened to find ourselves in central Africa instead of Manhattan at the very moment when all hell was breaking loose south of the Sahara?

No, it's not. It's not a coincidence at all.

I'd come to the Congo because one order was passing and a new one was taking its place. Europeans out, Africans in. A different crew was going to be calling the shots. The old rules and the cozy relationships that had prevailed for close to a century were obsolete overnight. Western idealists looked at this and thought about the exhilarating vistas of human devel-

21

opment that were opening up. My clients looked at it and thought, "It's payday for us."

So that's what brought me to Leopoldville with Sandy and Thomas tagging along.

All hell was breaking loose there for exactly the same reason. Old order passing, different crew, et cetera.

Katanga Province in the early sixties was producing 20 percent of all the world's copper and 80 percent of its cobalt. That was for starters. Not much happened in Detroit, Pittsburgh, Lyon, Frankfurt, or Yokohama without making cash registers ring in Katanga. Just mentioning the place made bankers, businessmen, and industrialists around the globe salivate.

The people running Katanga at the moment figured they should be the ones who decided what happened to this fabulous wealth that they'd been born on top of. The mining company officers got along very well with those people, and they figured the same thing. The rest of the Congo didn't think so. As soon as decolonization got the Belgian Army out of the way, the Congolese Defense Force and the Katanga *gendarmerie* hooked up in a first-rate civil war.

The United Nations sent in what with fine irony was called a "peacekeeping force." Europeans and Americans started seeing unfamiliar datelines like "Elizabethville" and "Jadotville" over breakfast every morning. By January of 1963, the peacekeepers had managed to kill some Katangans, and the dispatches said the rebellion had "unexpectedly collapsed." I tend to be suspicious of things that happen unexpectedly, but by late June I figured it was safe enough to risk the trip one of my French clients was screaming for.

About the same time, unfortunately, the UN ran short of money. The peacekeeping force was keeping peace mostly within a five-mile radius of Leopoldville and Stanleyville. In early July, after Thomas and Sandy started their vacation in Burundi, things got very interesting again in the Congolese countryside.

So it wasn't really coincidence that Thomas and Sandy and I were in roughly the same place at the same time as a group of Katangan guerrillas. We were all after the same thing, and in July 1963, central Africa was where it happened to be.

4

Lights out in Muramvya came about half an hour after sundown on July 7, when the soldiers shut off the auxiliary generator that served the inn. With the high summer moon still low on the horizon, the darkness had a deeper, more penetrating quality than Manhattanites ever experience in the big city. No street lights, no headlights, no neon. Inky blackness lit only by the cold brilliance of unimaginably distant stars enveloped the sleepy market town.

Just before midnight, nearly two hours after lying down on her cot, Sandy squirmed with a trace of irritation, certain that she hadn't gotten a particle of sleep and wasn't close to getting any. She glanced toward Thomas's cot, four feet away. She heard with confident familiarity the steady, regular breathing of his untroubled slumber.

Rising quietly from the cot, she picked her way through the brasserie and the silent lobby to the inn's front door. She stepped out onto the porch.

"Defense de sortir," a guard said firmly from the steps six feet away.

23

"Just a cigarette," Sandy answered coaxingly in French. She opened a pewter case and held it out to him. "You have one, too."

After hesitating for a moment, the soldier shifted his rifle to his left hand and took a Caporal from the case. Sandy took a cigarette for herself, put it between her lips, and let it dangle there, as she'd seen French soldiers do a thousand times, while she put the pewter case away and dug a waterproof matchbox from her pocket. She lit the soldier's cigarette first and then her own.

My apologies, by the way, to contemporary readers who find smoking distasteful. In 1963, the surgeon general's report was still a year away. Most New York grown-ups smoked. Sandy, who abstained during the day, pursued the habit more moderately than most of her peers. Adults who didn't smoke at all back then were regarded as either harmless eccentrics or prissy nuisances, depending on how much irritation they displayed when people around them lit up.

Leaning against the inn's front door, Sandy blew smoke at the porch ceiling and talked with the soldier in idiomatic, barrack-slang French about how long he'd been in the army, what French units he'd trained with, and how well his outfit had fought that day. He seemed very happy to discourse on these topics.

They had been talking for five or six minutes when a loud, explosive noise from one of the rooms on the gallery startled them. Reacting instinctively, the soldier rushed into the inn after an instant's frozen hesitation. Reacting reflectively, Sandy got rid of her cigarette and hit the porch floor facedown, flattening herself and kissing the dusty lumber. A veteran of colonial life and a survivor of the Algerian War, she knew that unarmed civilians running around where people were shooting at each other in the dark wouldn't contribute to anything but the casualty report.

Awake instantly at the explosive report, Thomas bolted up on his cot. Sensing Sandy's absence even in the total darkness, he verified it by slapping her empty cot. With quick, intense movements he dug the flashlight out of his knapsack and loped toward the doorway.

Uproar erupted on the gallery. In the pale flashlight beam,

24

Thomas could see soldiers converging from both directions on Room 1B. He heard emphatic banging on the door, and Ndala's voice shouting, *"Ouvrez!"*

"Light!" It was Mboya's voice, also on the gallery, shouting successively in several languages and eventually reaching English. "Whoever has that light, bring it to me at once."

Figuring that Sandy was as likely to be in that direction as any other, Thomas scurried compliantly toward the stairs.

From outside the back of the inn Thomas heard a muffled shout as he reached the gallery. Two shots close together, followed by a four-shot burst, came immediately after the shout. Each of those shots carried the distinctive, unmistakable double concussion—ka-*pow!*—of rifle fire.

Ndala stepped back from Room 1B's door and gestured impatiently to the soldiers around him. Two rifle butts slammed into the door, then immediately battered it again.

On television, those blows would've shattered the door to kindling so that the scene could be wrapped up in time for the next commercial. Real-world doors tend to be a bit more challenging, and this one remained stubbornly unyielding. Unlike a television detective of the era, Ndala didn't simply step forward and blow the lock off with his pistol, either. Television detectives don't have to worry about wounding their own men with ricocheting live ammunition, but Ndala did. The soldiers added their shoulders to the rifle butts and continued hammering away.

Sandy stayed exactly where she was. She was still lying on the porch two minutes later when she heard a scraping sound to her right. She glanced in that direction.

Two naked male legs appeared faintly in the moonlight below the porch roof. What was above the legs followed. A man in his birthday suit swung from the roof onto the porch, breathing hard, looking rapidly to his left, right, and behind him, running full tilt as soon as he hit the porch floor.

Sandy opened her mouth but didn't get a chance to yell. Moving at top speed in a barely controlled panic, the man didn't see her or give her time to warn him. One of his feet caught Sandy in the ribs, the other hit her bottom. With a surprised yelp, the man pitched headlong onto the floor.

Lying stunned for only a moment, he started to scramble

up. He looked in alarm toward the sound of running feet coming around the outside of the porch. He hadn't made it to his knees before a rifle muzzle eight inches from his head stopped him.

The soldier holding the rifle seemed to look in indecision from Sandy to the naked figure. But Claude Devereaux wasn't undecided. He knew the game was up. Collapsing on the porch floor, he swore in elaborate, blasphemous French.

Room 1B's door gave way at about the same moment. A soldier belly-flopped into the room, sweeping his rifle around the far half of it. A colleague, shoulder pressed against the outside of the doorjamb, covered the other half. Everyone in the hallway held his breath, waiting for a gunshot or a scream. Nothing happened.

Waving Thomas's flashlight, Mboya crowded to Ndala's side in the doorway. The beam swept briefly over the thoroughly ransacked room, then picked out the unmistakable sheen of blood-caked flesh and stopped.

The body lay prone on the bed against the room's right wall. White male, a bit under six feet tall, Thomas thought. Hole in the back of his head.

Coming to his feet, the soldier on the floor darted forward, rummaged through a disorderly pile of odds and ends near the front of the bed, and plucked what looked like a passport from it. He brought it to Ndala, who opened the booklet and held it at arm's length to get it in the glow from the flashlight.

"Alex Hanson," he read. "American."

5

"Major, you will if you please allow no further distur-
bance of this room until I have examined it," Mboya said. The
French words were deliberate and almost laboriously ar-
ticulated. As he finished, the inn's generator groaned back to
life and light flooded the interior of the building.

Apparently unimpressed by the coincidence, Ndala
snapped a response to Mboya in Kirundi. Thomas didn't understand a syllable of that, but the tone sounded less than
acquiescent.

"Excuse me, Major," Mboya replied, still in French. "I
agree that if this were a combat zone the matter would be
under military jurisdiction. Less than twelve hours ago, however, you dictated sleeping arrangements here based on your
determination that Muramvya was a secure area."

A hint of unpleasant recollection washing across his face,
Ndala started to speak and then stopped. Mboya continued.

"We are confronted with an apparent violation of Burundi
criminal law. There is no reason to believe that either the
victim or the possible perpetrator were involved in military

activity. The presumed crime is therefore a matter for civil jurisdiction. I must respectfully insist that you permit me to do my job."

Without waiting for any assent, Mboya started to move into the room. Ndala brusquely blocked his way, shouldering Mboya's muscular frame back into the hall where for an unbalanced moment he jostled Thomas. A burst of Ndala's clipped, rapid-fire Kirundi followed.

"You insist on preventing me from discharging my responsibility," Mboya said in French, completely unruffled. "Very well. I will take the matter up with my superiors, who will take it up with yours." He paused for a moment. "Meanwhile, I insist that you at least secure the room and leave it unmolested until we receive an answer from Bujumbura."

Again Ndala hesitated. He looked uncertainly from Mboya to Thomas. Then, swiveling his head, he ripped off a series of orders. A soldier swung the broken door shut and took up a position directly in front of it with his rifle at port arms.

Not exactly a win, Thomas thought. But a definite tie. When a civilian in a nightgown confronts a troop of armed soldiers and comes out of it with a draw, it's hard not to be impressed.

"You will come with me," Mboya said to Thomas. "Wait in the lobby while I put some clothes on." Then, as an afterthought, "If you please."

The first thing Thomas wanted to do was find Sandy, but instead of arguing he nodded and headed for the stairs. A tie deserved at least that much. More important, he figured that if he hadn't tracked Sandy down before Mboya showed up downstairs he could debate the issue then.

He didn't have to. Sandy was standing just inside the front door when Thomas squeezed past the soldier stationed at the bottom of the stairs. She glanced up at Thomas at the same moment he spotted her.

"There you are," Thomas said. "Someone named Alex Hanson's been killed upstairs. There's a presumed murderer running around somewhere."

"No longer, if you are referring to Devereaux," Sandy said. "He has been arrested."

"What stunning efficiency," Thomas said. "How did they manage that so quickly?"

"Haste makes waste," Sandy shrugged. "Devereaux was leaving in a hurry, and he tripped over a Frenchwoman."

"It happens to the best of us," Thomas sighed. "But that should make Mboya's job easier, anyway."

"Is Mboya investigating?" Sandy asked, surprised.

"He seems to think so, and I have a sneaking suspicion that I've been conscripted into his service. Mboya and Major Ndala had words on the subject. I think Mboya decided to enlist me."

"What makes you say that?"

"Ndala wanted to talk things over in Kirundi. Mboya did his side of the conversation in baby-French, to be sure I could understand it. And he kept repeating what Ndala had said so that I'd get the gist of the whole discussion."

"I see," Sandy said, her tone less than pleased. "He wanted a witness that Ndala could not intimidate as easily as he could a Burundian."

"You have misgivings?"

"Yes, since you ask." She seemed just short of cross. "I understand little of what is going on here, and I suspect you understand even less. I would have preferred for us to fade into the background."

"I don't blame you. If any Burundians are more intimidated by Ndala than I am they must be paralyzed with fear."

"But you have nevertheless—" Sandy began. She stopped talking as Mboya's bass tones cut through the lobby.

"Get this message on the radio immediately," Mboya was saying to the younger black man striding along behind him whom he had identified at the ambush site as a bureaucrat. "Do not let them put you off on any pretext. Do not send it from the command post. Go to the prefecture and talk to the constable on duty. Get him out of bed if you have to. Kick him in the rear if you have to."

Bobbing his head in response to each injunction, the younger man scurried off.

"Thank you for waiting, Monsieur Curry," Mboya said then as he came up to Thomas and Sandy. He thrust a pencil and a pad in a leatherette folder at Thomas. "You will need this. Come with me, please."

"I understand that Devereaux's been arrested," Thomas said, torn between Mboya's insistence and Sandy's disapproval.

"I understand the same thing," Mboya said, already halfway to the door. "And it was explained to me while I was dressing that Madame Curry was in a position to observe the arrest closely. You will perhaps ask her to write a précis of her observations as soon as she finds it convenient to do so. Now, if you please, we must hurry."

"He still has my flashlight," Thomas said apologetically to Sandy, as if this explained his decision to hustle after Mboya.

Mboya strode around the back of the inn, the flashlight beam playing on the base of the wall. Thomas had to scurry to keep up with him.

"Write this," Mboya said. "Drop from sill of Room 1B to ground, roughly five meters. A man of normal height hanging from the sill would— Wait a moment."

Thomas followed the flashlight beam as it left the wall and picked up a limp bundle on the ground. For a riveting moment, Thomas thought they'd found another corpse.

Mboya knelt beside the object. He spent two long minutes bathing it with light and gingerly poking it before he spoke. "Write this," he said then. "Shirt, male, one. Trousers, male, one pair. Pillow, one, stuffed inside them. Apparent bullet holes in shirt, four. Found at the base of the inn's rear wall, roughly one meter to the right of a direct vertical drop from the Room 1B windowsill."

Mboya was on his feet again, shining the flashlight on the back wall. Thomas scribbled furiously.

"Write this: Distance from sill of Room 1B window to roof approximately two meters."

Twenty more minutes of pacing, kneeling, squatting, and flashlighting produced only the instruction to write, "No further observation."

"I think we can go to the porch," Mboya said then.

"By all means," Thomas said.

Mboya grinned over his shoulder as he moved at a more leisurely pace around the corner.

"I am imposing on you, I know," he said.

"Not at all."

"My apologies. As soon as that eager young *fonctionnaire* is back from sending my radio message, I will press him into service in your place. But I did not want to lose time in the meanwhile."

"I understand."

They had reached the front of the inn. Light from inside amply illuminated the porch. Mboya clicked off the flashlight. Standing outside the railing at the far end, moving only his eyes, he began a systematic, square-inch by square-inch examination of the porch.

"The disruption of your plans must be extraordinarily frustrating," he said distractedly as he gazed at the porch floor. "It cannot have left you well disposed toward our poor country."

"If we'd wanted a Disneyland vacation we'd have gone to California," Thomas said. "We weren't looking for anything quite this exciting, I'll admit. But as long as it all comes out all right we'd be perverse to get upset about it. Back in New York we'll be able to have dinner on these stories for months."

"You are rather polite for an American, Monsieur Curry." Silent for a moment, Mboya then continued musingly. "Americans often confuse affability with politeness, just as the French tend to think they are being polite when they are merely being correct. Well. We will try to keep the inevitable inconvenience to you and Madame Curry from this point forward to a minimum."

" 'Inevitable inconvenience?' " Thomas asked warily.

"There is some still in store for you, I fear," Mboya said. "You and Madame Curry are witnesses. Potentially, you are very important witnesses."

"We'll be happy to give you statements and fly back for the trial if necessary," Thomas said.

"The trial is the least of it," Mboya commented. "Burundi inherited a continental system of criminal justice from the Belgian trustees imposed on us by the League of Nations and the UN. Rather different from the Anglo-Saxon

31

procedures you are familiar with. The key in our system is the judicial investigation."

"So I've heard," Thomas said.

"Doing that investigation properly can involve interviewing important witnesses many different times and may take rather longer than I or you would like."

"In concept perhaps," Thomas protested, "but how complicated can this be? There's—"

"Let me ask you a question, Monsieur Curry," Mboya said. "Where is the gun?"

"I beg your pardon?"

"An uncomplicated investigation assumes the following hypothesis: Around midnight, two men are in Room 1B of an inn known to be swarming with combat troops. One of them kills the other with a single pistol shot in the back of the head. Having done this remarkably stupid thing, the killer proceeds to behave very coolly and cleverly. He concludes that the only way to save his hide is to run. With soldiers beating down the locked door behind him, the killer nevertheless takes the time to pull his pants and shirt around a pillow and throw this makeshift mannequin from the window in a successful effort to distract the guard at the back of the inn. He then nimbly climbs onto the roof, scurries to the front of the inn, and acrobatically descends to the porch, counting on surprising and overpowering any guard he finds there and making his escape into the town and ultimately into the countryside. Am I right so far?"

"It sounds good to me."

"Well then, Monsieur Curry, where is the gun?"

"I think I see what you mean."

"Why would the killer leave the gun in the room or throw it away when there is so much other evidence against him that finding the gun on him would make little difference? Wouldn't a man running for his life instead hang onto the gun, which would come in very handy if he encountered some guard along the way who objected to his escape?"

"Perhaps he wasn't thinking very clearly."

"He was thinking clearly enough when he distracted the guard in back."

"All right," Thomas said, "I'll bite. Where's the gun?"

"I have no idea," Mboya said. "That is why I say this investigation may be more complicated than either of us perhaps thought at first. Much more complicated indeed."

6

"Did they eventually find the gun?" I asked Thomas over the crackling of ear-pricking static when he reached me by telephone that evening. He was phoning from a call box in a café next to the Hotel Spaak in Bujumbura, but the connection sounded like the call had been routed through the Ukraine.

"They did find the gun," he told me. "Mboya fished it out of a rain barrel just before 9 A.M. The rest of us cheered because that finished his on-site investigation and meant we could start the trip to Bujumbura. After about seven hours bouncing around the inside of some troop-trucks they got for us, I began to wonder if we should've been quite so enthusiastic about it."

"I can imagine," I said. "But I take it you ultimately arrived safe and sound and are now enjoying the finest accommodations Bujumbura has to offer."

"Yes. As a matter of fact the Hotel Spaak is very nice. But it would be much nicer if Sandy weren't edgy and a little put out with me on top of that. That's why I'm calling you, Theodore."

"You've lost me."

"This chap Mboya seems to have a continuing role in mind for Sandy and me in his investigation, and the investigation gives every promise of going on until the Washington Senators win a pennant. He's talking to Sandy right now, and he's given me an appointment for first thing tomorrow."

"Sounds like he's moving right along. Isn't that what you want?"

"I think Sandy's afraid that some of the Algerian adventures during my misspent youth might be misconstrued if they were to surface in this context. Could take a bit of explaining."

"Why should they surface? Why should any part of your background show up in the files of the Burundi police?"

"Sandy's sure that Mboya had directed an inquiry about both of us to the French Embassy immediately after the ambush, even before the murder. At any rate, she's developed a sharp interest in not prolonging our stay unduly. She'd like us to make our discreet contribution and move on to other things. Elsewhere."

"I see." I frowned at the receiver. What was I supposed to do about all this from Leopoldville? "I understand the United States has a perfectly good embassy in Bujumbura," I said then. "Have you contacted it?"

"As it happens I just spoke with an earnest young gent from there who seems to have gone to Brown or Cornell or someplace. Not Princeton, at any rate. He gave me a list of Bujumbura *avocats* who he assures me are all really top drawer. Also, he wished me luck."

"That sounds a bit insubstantial," I conceded. "Fair enough, Thomas. I'll see if I can generate anything useful at this end."

"Thank you, Theodore. I'm sure you'll think of something."

I wish I had your confidence, I thought as I hung up.

7

Our fears weren't quite groundless but they were misplaced, as Sandy was in the process of finding out.

Sandy was sitting in Mboya's airy office at the Palais de Justice in Burundi. Sunlight gilded the off-white walls and picked up glinting stone highlights in the white and maroon squares on the terrazzo floor.

Sandy sat across a bleached maple desk from Mboya himself and a male clerk who was busily preparing the *procès-verbal* for the interview. They had arrived in Bujumbura just over two hours before. Mboya had found two well-stuffed manila folders waiting for him, containing the information that his underlings had pulled together quickly in response to the radio messages Mboya had sent to them from the ambush site and then from Muramvya.

"You met your husband in Algeria, in the early stages of the late war there, did you not, Madame Curry?"

"Our first encounter with each other was in Algeria in 1955, after the rebellion there had begun, that is correct."

"What was Monsieur Curry doing in Algeria?"

"I cannot be certain. We did not truly come to know each other until several years later in New York."

"How curious. My understanding was that soldiers under your father's command had arrested Monsieur Curry."

"I was seventeen years old at the time. I would not necessarily be conversant with everything that happened during my father's discharge of his military responsibilities."

Mboya smiled warmly and folded his hands on top of the folder nearer him.

"Madame Curry, if your intention is to evade my questions by hairsplitting prevarication without actually lying, you have been successful thus far."

"I beg your pardon?" Sandy said icily.

"You and Monsieur Curry should be grateful to René Martine."

"And who is he?"

"He is a Belgian national holding a senior position with the *Union Minière* in Katanga Province in the Congo. According to a report that the French government has been kind enough to share with mine, Monsieur Martine some nine months ago supervised the delivery to Katangese rebels of sixty-three British manufacture, Second World War–vintage, .303-caliber rifles. He had the Katangans acknowledge receipt of these weapons, carefully noting the serial number of each one. Each of the terrorist weapons recovered after the attack yesterday came from that consignment."

"And so?" Sandy asked innocently.

"And so we have no grounds for suspecting that your husband's involvement in yesterday's incident was anything other than accidental."

"I should think not," Sandy said.

"The fact that after service with the American Army during the Korean War, your husband apparently became involved in arms-smuggling activities in Algeria," Mboya said, paging through one of the folders, "is a matter of no consequence to me. If I did not fear that it might offend you for me to say so, I would mention that in 1955 I was pulling for the Algerian nationalists myself."

"Thank you for sparing my feelings." Sandy's tone was dry, her expression not without humor.

"Therefore, I hope you will feel free to be completely candid with me. Not merely that you will avoid lying, but that you will be as open about what you know as you can be."

"In the written précis that I gave you," Sandy said, "I tried to include in as exhaustive a fashion as possible everything I knew about the events in question."

"For which I thank you. It appears most thorough."

"There is also this," Sandy said. From her handbag she removed a small, silver, screw-top film canister and handed it to Mboya.

"'This' being what?" Mboya asked as he accepted it.

"The roll of film that was actually in the camera when the gunshot hit it during the ambush. I discovered after we got to Bujumbura that I had mistakenly given Major Ndala the previous day's roll of film when he approached me yesterday."

Mboya beamed, clenching the film can like a prize.

"Do you think the major will discover your mistake?" he asked.

"When he discovers thirty-six frames of elephants, his suspicions may well be aroused."

"You are giving this to me as a token of your trust," Mboya said. "You are suggesting that I should accept your candor at face value. It is a very subtle move on your part."

"So," Sandy shrugged. "What else can I tell you?"

"Why did you get up late last night and go out on the porch?"

Sandy sensed that the interrogation had reached a critical point. She had to decide whether to answer with the candor Mboya had asked for or resort again to what he'd correctly called prevarication.

Sandy accepted none of Mboya's honeyed assurances about not suspecting Thomas. She assumed that Mboya would cheerfully have lied through his teeth about that if he thought lying were the best way to extract information from her. At the same time, she thought, Mboya's inquiries to the French Embassy had obviously borne fruit, and he already knew about Algeria and Thomas's questionable activities there. She wanted to make Mboya believe that she and Thomas had nothing to hide. On tactical and not moral grounds she decided to tell him the truth.

"I was concerned about exactly the topic you just alluded to," she said. "I feared that a misguided connection might be drawn between what Thomas was accused of doing in Algeria eight years ago and what happened yesterday. To explore that possibility, I wanted to find out from the guard as much as I could about the attack. I hoped I would be able to figure out whether suspicion might conceivably fall on Thomas."

"And what did you learn?"

"I learned that the helicopters were in the air before daylight. The Katangan ambushers thought they were setting a trap, but in fact they were falling into one."

"And what significance do you attribute to this?"

"*Evidemment,* the terrorist attack was known in advance. If the attack was known, the people behind it were also known. Thomas and I were making open preparations with a registered guide in Bujumbura to go into the countryside at a time when the Burundi military almost certainly was preparing to meet the very attack that occurred. Had there been any fear that Thomas was involved in some way with the terrorists, we surely would not have been allowed to roam freely in an area where we might have warned the attackers about the trap they were walking into. For that matter, we probably would not have been allowed to enter Burundi in the first place."

"A compelling argument. Are you certain that gathering this useful information from the guard was your only reason for going out?"

"Of course I am certain."

"If I told you that Laurent Dray was stopped at a checkpoint two kilometers east of the town around 11:30 that evening, a little over half an hour before you went out on the porch, your answer would not change?"

"It would not."

"Good," Mboya said. "You did not indignantly demand to know what I was implying or pretend to be shocked. I appreciate that."

"I understand precisely what you were implying. Your implications may irritate me, but they are not likely to shock me."

"I very much hope that that is true, Madame Curry. Because I need your help."

"In what way?"

"Claude Devereaux has asked to see you."

"Why should he do that?" Sandy demanded, after a moment's surprise.

"I can only speculate."

"What is your speculation?"

"That he suspects a white European will listen to him with more sympathy than a Tutsi would," Mboya said. ("Tutsi" is the singular form of "Watusi.")

"Is he right?" Sandy asked.

"That would depend on the European and the Tutsi."

"I suppose it would," Sandy admitted. For the first time in the interview her smile showed a hint of warmth.

"What is intriguing is the fact that he thinks a sympathetic ear might be of some use to him. On the surface, his situation appears hopeless. Who else but he could possibly have committed the crime? What conceivable defense could he have to a charge of shooting a sleeping man in the back of the head? Yet, he seems to believe he has a story that should be examined. Why?"

"I have no idea," Sandy said.

"Nor will I—until I hear the story."

"I will not betray him," Sandy said. "If he tells me something in confidence, I will not repeat it to you."

"And I will not ask you to."

"If that is true, then what use can I be to you in this connection?"

"Simply knowing that Monsieur Devereaux does have a story, regardless of what it is, will be useful to me," Mboya said. "I cannot imagine any hypothesis under which he might be innocent. But if there is some explanation for why or how he committed this crime that he is willing to tell to you and not to me, then confirming that possibility will help me get at the whole truth about this affair. Which happens to be my job."

"In other words," Sandy said, "you wish to use me and to exploit whatever trust Devereaux wishes to place in me so that you may advance your investigation, whether it helps Devereaux or not."

"Precisely." Mboya beamed. "We understand each other perfectly."

40

"Why in the world would you expect me to agree to such a thing?"

"First of all, because nothing you do could possibly hurt Devereaux. His situation could not get any worse than it already is. The possibility that you will help him is admittedly slim, but it is the only chance he has. Second, because a person of your background and character could not turn down such a request from someone like Devereaux."

"What do you mean by that?" Sandy asked.

"I assume that you never saw Devereaux in your life until yesterday morning. But Devereaux was in the foreign legion, and you are the daughter of a French army officer who devoted much of his career to colonial service. In a sense, you have known Devereauxs all your life—all of those legionnaire rankers who served in the same places your father did, places where you grew up, formed your values, shaped your view of the world. I know the European colonial mindset, Madame Curry. I have spent my entire life learning it firsthand. Devereaux has a claim on you that I do not think you can refuse."

Sandy was silent for almost a minute after absorbing this assessment from the imposing black man before her.

"I will have to consult with Thomas," she said at last.

"Excellent. You would not consult with him if the answer were going to be negative, you know. You would simply have turned me down."

8

"Imagine Maryland. Roughly. Scrambled eggs and sausage—links, not patties."

P. Stuart Gallatin, commercial attaché at the United States Embassy in the Congo, spoke the first three words to me and the rest to the buffet attendant at the Belgian Armed Forces Commissary, which in 1963 was one of the best places in Leopoldville to get breakfast.

"Maryland, huh?" I already had a croissant and orange juice and a healthy respect for Gallatin's metabolism.

"Right. Ten percent, maybe 15 percent more people, but about the same size. Except, imagine Maryland without Baltimore or Annapolis or even Frederick, with 97 percent of all those people spread out over the countryside on tiny plots of land, doing subsistence farming and growing exactly one cash crop."

"Coffee?"

"No, thanks, I'm having tea," Gallatin said. "Oh, you mean Burundi's cash crop. Right. Coffee."

I shook my head as we found seats at a long table. Com-

42

mercial attaché humor is hard to take at seven-thirty in the morning. If you got right down to it, Gallatin in general was hard to take, but he was the only American diplomat in the Congo that I'd had much contact with so far, so I figured I had to start with him.

"How's that deal you're working on coming?" Gallatin asked.

"We're at the wait-and-see stage."

"Mmm. Any reason you couldn't find a piece of it for an American company?"

"Yes. The company that's engaged me for that purpose happens to be French. Lawyers aren't allowed to have clients with conflicting interests."

Gallatin shrugged away this technicality as he brought immense dignity to the task of transferring scrambled eggs to his mouth with a tin mess-kit fork.

"So Burundi must be an incredibly poor country if the only commodity it can sell internationally is coffee," I prompted.

"Desperately poor. Not a linear foot of railroad track in the entire place. Very few paved roads outside Bujumbura."

"Hm," I said.

"Not that I'm suggesting," Gallatin added pointedly, cocking an eyebrow at me, "that you can buy anyone in the government for a hundred and fifty bucks."

"That's not the approach I prefer," I assured him. "I'm not interested in having some African bureaucrat in my pocket. I'm just trying to keep two friends of mine from getting tangled up in red tape."

"Easier said than done."

"I don't see why it should be that big a deal. I'm not trying to spring them from a criminal charge or get them a license to remove ancient antiquities. They're potential witnesses in a murder case, they're making full and complete statements, the case is open and shut anyway, and they'll fly back to testify if they're needed. So the pitch is, let them be on their way. I'd think a phone call from the embassy'd be enough to swing it."

"Not from our embassy."

"Why not?"

"We're not the key foreign player in Burundi."

43

"Who is?"

"Your buddies the French."

"How did that happen?" I asked. "I thought Burundi was a Belgian trust area."

"Right. Which means French is an official language, along with whatever they call the Bantu dialect they speak over there. France's policy is to develop a special relationship with any country where French is an important diplomatic or commercial language. They're putting their buttons in that area."

"We have a lot more buttons than France does."

"Sure," Gallatin said. "And a lot more places to put them. We're busy saving the world from the Red menace. We can't screw around with some country that won't have strategic importance unless somebody figures out how to make rocket fuel out of coffee beans."

"So we don't have any hook at all?"

"Sure we have a hook."

"What is it?"

"I just told you. Coffee."

"What about coffee?" I asked, wishing I had some.

"Starting this year, coffee will be marketed internationally through a cartel called the International Coffee Convention that the UN just invented. Quotas are assigned to all sellers. You with me so far?"

"Yes." There may have been just the tiniest trace of asperity in my voice. I suspect there was, because Gallatin smiled.

"Okay. The votes on each side of the cartel are weighted by the volume of coffee transactions undertaken by the voting country. Americans drink a whole lot of coffee. We import most of it. So the United States has two-thirds of the votes on the buyers' side of the cartel."

"That sounds like a working majority," I said.

"If we care enough to vote, we'll generally win," Gallatin nodded.

"So if we vote at the next quota session that Burundi can't sell any coffee internationally next year, then they're stuck with their whole crop?"

"Minus what they can smuggle and drink themselves.

44

That's right. No hard currency. Very bad situation for a country that's only been independent for a little over a year."

"Then why wouldn't a phone call from the embassy carry some clout?" I insisted.

"No credibility. The Burundians aren't going to believe that we'd cut their coffee off over a couple of rich tourists who're inconvenienced because they have to consume the local culture for a couple more months than they'd planned on. After all, America wants to have as much coffee on the market as possible. Drives the price down."

"So?" I said. "They'd have to be convinced, that's all."

"No one on this side of the ocean can speak with that kind of conviction. We're talking about your basic Washington decision here. Do you suppose you could talk Dean Rusk and Luther Hodges into dropping everything else and looking into this option on an emergency basis?"

"No. I don't expect the secretary of state and the secretary of commerce to plan their days around my clients' problems."

"Probably right," Gallatin said sagely.

"Then what do you suggest?"

"Well, now that you know about this coffee business, I suppose you could try to bluff them yourself if they give you too hard a time."

"How much credibility would that have?"

"That'd depend on what happened when they looked into it."

I thought that over for a few seconds.

"Would they check a bluff like that with our embassy in Bujumbura or their own embassy in Washington?" I asked.

"Neither one. You're not paying attention. They'd check with their new pals, the French."

"So what good does that do me?" I was playing dumb. I could see it coming right down Broadway now, but I wanted to hear him say it.

"I know who the French informer assigned to our embassy here is," Gallatin said.

"The French are spying on us?"

"You bet. Ever since DeGaulle started being an asshole. Anyway, it wouldn't be hard for me to leave a cable draft

45

talking about the coffee option some place where this guy could find it.''

"That'd be very accommodating of you. I'd appreciate it.''

"What would be very accommodating of you,'' Gallatin said, "would be to find some way to cut a couple of American firms in on this action you're trying to hustle over here.''

"Didn't we already have this conversation?''

"You know, it seems like I spend every working hour trying to grub up 'Made in the U.S.A.' business in this intriguing part of the world. Doesn't leave much time for anything else. But if you came through on this construction deal, that'd free up enough time for me to get to work on the cable draft. By the way, thanks for the breakfast.''

I stood up long enough to shake hands with Gallatin and wish him a pleasant day. Then I sat back down to think about this disturbing conversation.

What bothered me wasn't Gallatin asking me to sell out my client. He was just doing his job. My client's taxes weren't paying his salary. If I could be had I was fair game.

What bothered me was all the stuff about what bad guys the French were. I'd seen some newspaper reports about real friction developing between the French and American governments, but I'd assumed it was mostly posturing for public consumption in France. If the professionals were taking it seriously, though, there must be a lot more to it.

Thomas had said Sandy was edgy and a bit put out with him. Gallatin's little shots had left *me* feeling vaguely uncomfortable about divided loyalties, and I'd been practicing international law for over ten years. I knew the rules backward and forward. But knowing the rules doesn't make something feel right in your gut. With things coming together in the inconvenient way they were, I wondered if Sandy was suddenly having to deal with emotional conflicts exponentially greater than mine.

I didn't realize it until about twenty-four hours later, but it was really at that moment that I decided to fly to Bujumbura.

9

"You left Princeton University in October of your senior year and enlisted in the United States Army, which was in the midst of the Korean War," Mboya said to Thomas as he paged through the file before him. "The timing seems odd. Would you care to explain it?"

"What in the world does that have to do with Alex Hanson's murder?" Thomas asked.

"If I knew the answer to that question," Mboya explained, smiling patiently, "I would probably also know the answer to the question I asked. Are you reluctant to discuss the matter?"

"My mother always told me that it was ill-bred to talk about yourself."

"Then I shall have to exercise my ingenuity to see if I can imagine some relevance for my inquiry," Mboya said. He leaned back in his swivel chair and stroked the lapel of his charcoal gray suit. "Let me see. According to the army report on the engagement two days ago, four of the terrorists were confirmed dead. As a former helicopter pilot in Korea, what is your reaction to that information?"

47

"Surprise."

"Why?"

As he considered the question, Thomas played for a moment with the Pentax camera that Mboya had retrieved from Ndala and returned to Thomas at the beginning of the interview.

"When a properly trained airborne assault force takes on ground troops without air cover, the result should be a massacre, not a battle," Thomas said after a second's reflection. "The ground troops can either die while they run or die where they sit. They don't really have any other options."

"Do you know who Kerry Travis is?" Mboya asked abruptly.

"No."

"Pity. No one else does either. I thought you might."

"Why?"

"He is an American," Mboya shrugged. "He was the only white person missing after the attack on the convoy. He had the bad luck to hitch a ride on one of the trucks instead of simply taking the bus. There are relatively few Americans in Burundi. I thought you might have run across him during your stay here."

"He seems to have succeeded in avoiding us."

"Let me see, then. In light of your well-bred reluctance to discuss yourself and the limits of my own imagination, I will not ask you about resigning from the staff of the United States Attorney for the Southern District of New York, or about your colorful experiences before then in Algeria—both topics on which the French government found it useful to inform itself during the decade just past, and about which it kindly informed mine when your name first came up."

"Ah, those malicious rumors," Thomas sighed.

"The gunrunning was only a rumor?"

"Gunrunning was never actually proven, was it?"

"That depends on what you mean by 'proven,'" Mboya said.

"I suppose it does at that," Thomas said.

"Let me just verify the remainder of the information that my zealous assistants have gathered. After returning from overseas, you completed your undergraduate work at New

48

York University rather than Princeton—less prestigious, no?''

''Less expensive also.''

''I see. Expense was a concern because you had not yet received your mother's bequest?''

''Exactly.''

''Even though she seems to have died many years before.''

''My mother was killed in 1949 when a Red Chinese shell blew up the International Red Cross warehouse where she was working in Nanking.''

''I am sorry to hear it. But the bequest—''

''My mother was a careful woman. The trust fund she left to me didn't vest until I turned twenty-nine.''

''Very well. You received your law degree from Columbia, joined the U.S. attorney's staff—I suppose that made us colleagues, in a sense—left the U.S. attorney's office, and then you were disbarred, am I right?''

''You are not.''

''In what respect am I mistaken?''

''I was not disbarred. I voluntarily surrendered my license to practice law.''

''Thank you for correcting me, Monsieur Curry.'' Mboya used a large fountain pen to make a notation on the top page in the file. ''Lawyers must be precise, mustn't they?''

10

" 'To the commandant of Sainte Jeanne Military Prison,' " Thomas read, translating a bit haltingly from French as he did so, the stiff, official paper crinkling in his fingers. " 'Greetings. Claude Devereaux having been duly tried'—Sandy, what does *'par contumace'* mean?"

" '*In absentia.*' "

" '—having been duly tried *in absentia* for and convicted of unlawful acts impairing the state security of the Kingdom of Burundi, and said unlawful acts having been committed in a combat zone under military jurisdiction at the time of the offense, and the said Claude Devereaux having accordingly been sentenced to be passed under arms by reason of the same, now, therefore, you are hereby commanded, at such time as the said Claude Devereaux shall have been delivered into your custody, to hold him in close confinement until 15 July 1963, and as soon as convenient after first light on such date cause him to be put to death by musketry.' Signed Michel Ndala, Officer Commanding, First Military District."

" 'By musketry'?" Sandy asked, arching her eyebrows at Devereaux as she repeated the quaint term.

"Exact. It was their rather tiresome way of saying I was to be shot instead of hanged. Because of it being a military jurisdiction instead of a civil one and so forth."

The three of them were standing in Devereaux's three-square-meter cell at the Saint Sulpice Civil Crimes Confinement Facility in Bujumbura. Thomas and Sandy stood near the outside wall so that sunlight filtering through the grilled window behind them would fall on the death warrant from which Thomas had just read. Devereaux leaned against the floor-to-ceiling bars opposite them. Thomas had finished his interview with Mboya not quite two hours before.

Devereaux carefully examined Thomas's features as Thomas read through the brief document. The tanned face was angular, his expression suggesting affected boredom masking intelligent curiosity. The carefully trimmed mustache matched brown hair beginning to creep over the tops of his ears, a little longer than most American men wore their hair in 1963. Devereaux thought at first that he'd read impatience in the green-flecked brown eyes, but he decided now that it was instead irritation, mixed with a trace of tension.

Soft, he thought. Soft, rich, pampered American. Certainly does not deserve the spirited *française* he has somehow acquired.

"In short," Sandy said to Devereaux, nodding toward the death warrant that Thomas still held, "you had a good reason to kill Alex Hanson, who apparently was staying at the Muramvya Inn under the assumed identity of Terence Donoghue."

"Hypothetically, I suppose you are right," Devereaux said. "Let me see, how would it go? I was a fugitive. Hanson could have recognized me and threatened to turn me in unless I came up with a bribe I was unable or unwilling to produce. The obvious solution to this dilemma was to lock myself in a room with Hanson in an inn surrounded by soldiers and then kill him in the loudest and most attention-getting manner possible."

"I think not," Sandy said, not in the least offended by Devereaux's biting sarcasm. "Hanson need not have known you were a fugitive. After all, Mboya apparently did not. Even if Hanson had known your status, it would have been very

51

foolhardy of him not to denounce you immediately. Only an optimist would assume that he had a better chance of collecting a bribe than a bullet from a man on the run."

"Then why did I kill him?"

"You needed his money, possibly also his gun. More important, you discovered that he had a passport among his effects that he had not turned over to the innkeeper, and you desperately needed that. You waited until he was asleep, hoping to make away with these items. As you did so, however, he woke up and discovered you. You panicked and shot him."

Devereaux smiled, nodding in at least feigned appreciation of the theory's elegance.

"But my state of undress at the critical time presents an inconvenient inconsistency, *d'accord?*"

"No. You had already made up the improvised mannequin that you used to distract the outside guard's attention. You had decided that you needed clothes less than you needed the diversion."

"And why did I shoot Monsieur Hanson instead of clubbing him over the head or doing something else less calculated to attract attention?"

"Because you had not planned to kill him originally, but lost your head in the panic of the moment. Besides, Hanson was a good-sized man. Once he had awakened, you could not be certain of overpowering him."

"She has me," Devereaux said to Thomas, slapping his palms on his thighs at the climax of an exaggerated shrug. *"Evidemment,* I am guilty. The investigation is a mere exercise, and the trial will be a formality. Everyone would save time by proceeding immediately to the execution."

"Bien," Sandy said, a touch of impatience marring her voice. "If I am wrong, tell me why."

"I did not kill Alex Hanson."

"Who did?"

"I do not know."

"This should be good," Thomas said to Sandy. Then, looking back at Devereaux, he said, "Tell us what happened."

"Hanson did not seem as upset as I would have expected him to be when the soldiers informed him that Ndala had expropriated half of his room for my benefit. We talked off and

52

on in the course of the afternoon about nothing in particular. He gave me some of his dried dates—far better than any other food available at the inn, by the way."

"I can believe that," Thomas said.

"At all events, I was very tired even before lights out. I went to sleep on a blanket and pillow that he provided to me while he kept the bed for himself."

"Then what happened?" Sandy prompted.

"The next thing I remember is an explosive, head-splitting noise close by that instantly woke me up with my ears ringing. There was no light in the room, but I could smell powder in the air. I jumped up in the dark. My eardrums were screaming, and my head felt as if it were bouncing off the walls. The moment I put my hands on Hanson I was certain he was dead. By then, soldiers were hammering at the door."

"But you weren't inclined to let them in?" Thomas asked.

"I confess that I did not view my prospects as brilliant. I was already officially a military fugitive. I had no desire to be shot 'resisting arrest,' which I am morally certain is what would have happened if I had opened the door."

"The soldier who actually arrested you did not shoot you," Sandy pointed out.

"Only because you were there, madame," Devereaux said.

"So you ran instead," Thomas said.

"Correct. I knew I was as good as dead if I jumped out the window to the ground. Therefore, I put the dummy together quickly, used that to draw the guard's fire, and made my way out over the roof. Had it not been for Madame Curry's accidental presence on the porch, I would have been in the countryside by dawn and either dead or in the Congo the following day."

"The shot woke you up," Sandy said, "but not fast enough to see the person who fired the shot make his own escape?"

"I saw nothing the moment I woke up but the faint outline of the window."

"Apparently, then," Thomas said, "you were set up."

"*Evidemment,*" Devereaux snapped.

"But you have no idea in the world who did it, or why, or how it was accomplished?"

"Correct."

"Okay. Now tell us the rest."

"I have told you everything, I think," Devereaux said after a moment's unpleasant surprise.

"*Je crois que non,*" Thomas said, deliberately exaggerating his less-than-accomplished American pronunciation of the French phrase. "For example, what did Major Ndala get you sentenced to death for?"

"Inasmuch as I thought it the better part of prudence to avoid the trial, I cannot be certain. I rather suspect that it was something about selling militarily useful information to hostile elements. That is the customary charge in situations like mine."

" 'Hostile elements?' " Sandy asked. "You mean the Katangan terrorists?"

"No. I mean the Hutus."

"Is there some kind of trouble brewing among them?" Thomas pressed.

"Nothing immediate as far as I know. But imagine that in North America there were nine Indians for every white, and the whites held the same degree of power that they do now. The whites would be habitually anxious about the situation, *d'accord?*"

"At a minimum," Thomas agreed.

"That is the way it has been in Burundi since independence. From the Watusi perspective, all Hutus are hostile elements by definition. The Watusi see a bloody Hutu uprising lurking behind every meeting between a Hutu and a white, every rumor of an arms shipment, every hint of unrest. The Watusi spend a lot more time worrying about them than about Katangan terrorists."

"Were you selling sensitive information to them?" Sandy asked.

"Why should I?" Devereaux snorted. "Assuming I had any, they couldn't afford to buy it."

"What do you suppose gave Major Ndala's court-martial the impression that you were?" Thomas wondered innocently.

"Neither Ndala nor the officers on the court-martial imagined that I was doing any such thing."

"If Ndala nevertheless framed you for that crime," Sandy said, "why did he do it?"

Devereaux hesitated for a moment, glancing from Thomas to Sandy. Then he folded his arms across his chest and answered Sandy's question.

"I suspect he was upset about a financial transaction in which we were both involved."

"A tantalizing response that rather begs for details," Thomas said.

"Unfortunately," Devereaux said, "details take time and time is something we do not have."

"Is one of those details by any wild chance Kerry Travis?" Thomas demanded.

"I am not familiar with anyone by that name," Devereaux answered instantly. "Monsieur Curry, if you wish to believe I was spying for the Hutus, you are free to do so. It would be an enterprise rather nobler than many that have been imputed to me. The important point for the moment is that I did not kill Alex Hanson."

"Why did you ask to see me?" Sandy asked then.

"Have you ever seen anyone executed by firing squad, madame?"

"No, but I will accept on faith that it is a thoroughly disagreeable experience."

"I have had the opportunity. They were always the same. Three privates and a sergeant. The privates always looked bored. The sergeant would line the privates up five meters from a concrete wall, stand the prisoner against the wall, step aside, shout three orders, and that was that. It took less than two minutes and had all the romance of kitchen duty. The volley would literally lift the condemned man off his feet and slam him against the wall before he pitched forward onto his face. If he was still breathing, the sergeant would finish him off with his pistol."

"It sounds every bit as unpleasant as I would have imagined," Thomas said.

"All that was absolutely normal," Devereaux said. "What was hard was seeing the expression on the prisoners'

55

faces. There was something even worse than fear that none of them could hide. I think it was disappointment. I could almost hear them thinking as they took their last look around the dingy cellar and saw the privates in their fatigues, 'Is this it? Is this all there is to it?' "

"One could sympathize with their position," Sandy said.

"I had complete contempt for their position," Devereaux retorted. "What did they expect? A sun-washed parade ground? Officers in dress whites? A band playing the death march? Compatriots witnessing the martyrdom, dabbing their eyes and silently vowing to continue the struggle? Is that what they thought they'd get out of Marxism or nationalism or whatever other stupid 'ism' they were throwing their lives away for?"

"Your point being, I take it," Thomas said, "that you would very much prefer to avoid dying the dreary, pointless death you found so contemptible when it was suffered by others."

"Close, Monsieur Curry. I cheerfully accept the risk that I will die in a prison basement, at the end of a rope or on the wrong side of a firing squad. But if I die that way, I'm not going to die for some schoolboy political theory. I'm going to die for something sensible. I'm going to die for money."

"You are saying," Sandy interjected, "that you asked to talk to me because you are truly innocent of Alex Hanson's murder, whatever else you may have done. You do not trust Mboya to exculpate you, and you think that somehow I can help."

"Exact. I am not asking you to undertake your own investigation or do anything heroic."

"What are you asking?" Thomas demanded.

"Two things. One, that you give careful thought to anything you might have seen or heard during the episode that seems significant in light of what I have said, and that you pass it on to Mboya. Two, that you let Mboya know someone is scrutinizing his conduct of the investigation."

"Why should he care that I am keeping an eye on him?" Sandy asked, amused by the thought.

"Because you are French. You are an educated product of the society whose culture pervades Mboya's own. He cares about your approval at least as much as he does that of his superiors. Because you were on the scene, you are in a better position than most people to know whether he is truly trying to find out what happened or is cutting corners and doing whatever the soldiers tell him to do."

"Fair enough," Sandy said. "But if that is the role you have in mind for me, why do you expect Mboya to cooperate with it—by letting us see you, for example?"

"Because he expects me to reveal things to you that I would not tell him and that will help him in his investigation."

"I have already told him that I will disclose nothing you tell me in confidence."

"No doubt," Devereaux nodded. "Mboya believes he is better at extracting information than you are at concealing it. He is probably right."

"That's why you're not burdening us with any details about the background to this adventure?" Thomas offered.

"Correct," Devereaux shrugged. "Neither intentionally nor inadvertently can you reveal what you do not know."

"How you had avoided arrest, how you came to be traveling in the same party as a senior *juge d'instruction* even though you were a fugitive, what the full story between you and Ndala is, why Ndala didn't simply place you under arrest the moment he saw you after the ambush—these all fall into the detail category, is that it?" Thomas asked.

"For now, at least."

"And you are certain that you have told us everything that you know about the shooting of Hanson?" Sandy asked.

"Absolutely certain. Upon my honor as a gentleman and a veteran of the foreign legion."

He's lying through his teeth, Sandy thought.

11

"He's lying through his teeth," Thomas said.

"*D'accord,*" Sandy answered absently as she continued to doodle on a table napkin that, unfolded, seemed to approach the dimensions of a baby blanket. She and Thomas were sitting at a metal latticework table shaded by a massive red and white umbrella on the Hotel Spaak's patio, looking out over the muddy brown water of Lake Tanganyika. Lake Tanganyika is big—think of Massachusetts and most of Connecticut under four thousand feet of water—so there was plenty to look it.

"*Tant pis pour nous,*" Thomas said. "We have to help him anyway."

"*We* do not have to do anything of the sort," Sandy said. She stopped sketching long enough to take a sip of Chablis.

His ears pricking up at the pronoun, Thomas decided to change the subject.

"I thought only officers in the foreign legion could be French, and all the rankers had to come from other countries," he said.

"Please do not change the subject," Sandy said. "You

were put out with me for even wanting to see Devereaux, and you were quite right."

"What irritated me a bit, actually, was your reversal of position. It upset you when I let Mboya pull me into the middle of things in Muramvya, but then the next thing I know you're letting him do exactly the same thing to you here."

"Distinction without a difference," Sandy said. "The point is, you were correct. It was an error for me to involve you further in this affair, when I should have—"

"The point is I was wrong," Thomas said. "After I'd thought it through, I realized why you felt you should go along with what Mboya asked. Your reasoning was perfectly sound."

"Of course it was. But that has nothing to do with involving you."

"It has plenty to do with involving us."

"That does not follow," Sandy insisted.

"You know better than that. You quit a job in a foreign country because otherwise you would've betrayed your father's friends or your country or yourself. The principle here is exactly the same."

Sandy slapped the table with her left hand. A Chablis wavelet lapped over the side of her wine glass.

"That is an extremely exasperating argument," she snapped.

"Those are generally the best kind," Thomas nodded.

"All Mboya has asked me to do is talk to Devereaux and report anything I can that might shed more light on what really happened. That is simple enough for me to do without assistance—from you or anyone else."

"All you were *asked* to do," Thomas said. "I notice you didn't say all you intended to do."

"I would prefer not to be cross-examined."

"It was an observation, not a question."

"It was an observation reflecting an unwarranted assumption."

"The assumption is warranted by the fact that you are a formidable woman who isn't likely to accept passively roles assigned to you by a bureaucrat or an adventurer—"

"Or a husband."

59

"—and by the fact that throughout this little chat you have been busily sketching a floor plan of the inn at Muramvya."

"Thomas, you tend to become particularly infuriating during these periodic attacks of cleverness."

"So I have been told. By the way, *can* a Frenchman enlist in the ranks of the foreign legion?"

"If he claims to be Belgian he can," Sandy said crisply, standing up. "I am going for a walk. I will see you back at the room half an hour before dinner."

Thomas rose as Sandy gathered the doodled floor plan into her purse.

"I'm correct in surmising that you'd prefer to take your stroll alone?"

"Your inferential powers are undiminished," Sandy said as she swept away.

Thomas watched her back all the way to the stairs.

12

I have no idea why, but in 1963 there was one American tobacco product you could be absolutely certain of buying anywhere in the world where French was spoken. Five minutes after Sandy had disappeared, Thomas paid the bill for her wine and his scotch and went through the hotel's rear entrance to its news and tobacco counter to take advantage of this cross-cultural phenomenon.

"Two Daniel Webster cigars," he said. "And an *International Herald Tribune*." Then, as an afterthought, "Oh. And a roll of thirty-five-millimeter color slide film."

"*Pellicule* preent onliment," the attendant said.

"Print film will be fine if that's all you have," Thomas said, after taking a moment to decipher the patois franglais.

"Try*expan* onliment," he said then. *"Pas de couleur."*

"Black-and-white will do nicely. I prefer it, actually. Captures more texture and resonance than all that distracting color. I'm sorry I didn't ask for Tri-X Pan in the first place."

A dubious expression dominating his face, the attendant took Thomas's money and slid his purchases across the counter to him. Thomas thanked him, put the cigars in the inside pocket of his pale blue, summer-weight blazer, folded the newspaper over the yellow box of film, and headed for the elevator that would take him to the second floor, where he and Sandy shared a front suite.

"Please come in and make yourself comfortable," Laurent Dray said to Sandy, about fifteen minutes after Thomas's transaction. He swept his arm around the exiguous storefront office that served as the headquarters for his guide business. "Your appearance is the only agreeable aspect of what has thus far been a distinctly unpleasant day."

"Unpleasant in what respect?" Sandy asked as she seated herself on a dusty, overpadded, chrome and vinyl chair that looked like it had been salvaged from a Baltic airport lounge.

"In the respect principally that I have had the dubious pleasure of several hours' transcribed conversation with Magistrate Mboya. He was highly critical of the fact that I had left a touring party unattended overnight. He received my account of my movements that evening with pronounced skepticism. And most annoying of all, he insinuated that I might be involved in some sort of compromising relationship with you, madame."

"What an absurd notion," Sandy said.

"I explained as much."

"You must have been quite insulted."

"Wounded to the depths of my soul, I assure you," Dray said in a less than deeply injured tone. "Of course, I would have denied it even if it had been true."

"A contingency irrelevant to my present purpose," Sandy said.

"Which is what?"

"To learn about an American named Kerry Travis."

"According to Magistrate Mboya," Dray said, "this Travis was missing following the attack on the convoy."

"I am interested in information about him according to Monsieur Dray."

Taking a gold-filled cigar case out of the deep breast pocket on his shirt, Dray opened it and offered it to Sandy. She shook her head, murmuring "No, thank you" as she did so.

Dray selected a small cigar from the case and spent about thirty seconds on the ritual of getting it lit. Sandy closed her eyes as she savored for a moment the rich, sweet aroma of the smoke. She thought she might try a cigar sometime. In private.

"I do not have a great deal of information about him," Dray said. "The American community in Bujumbura is very small, self-contained, spends 99 percent of its time within a one-kilometer radius of the western embassies' compound. I do not think Travis devotes much attention to that community. I have seldom run into him over there."

"What do you know about him?"

Dray shrugged.

"He apparently supports himself without doing anything that looks very much like work. This implies that he makes himself useful to some people in the Burundi ruling class. How or who or in what specific way I do not know."

"In other words, he lives on his income, as Devereaux said about himself," Sandy offered.

"Devereaux," Dray snorted. "Claude Devereaux spends most of his time in bars cultivating an air of intrigue as if Alain Delon or Sidney Greenstreet were about to walk through the door in a trench coat. In reality, he is a cheap *flic-indicateur* and a glorified errand boy for some of the more political soldiers."

"You have told all this to Mboya?" Sandy asked.

"Mboya knows it as well as I do."

"Then why would Mboya not have known when Devereaux was traveling with him on the convoy that Devereaux was a fugitive under a court-martial's death sentence?"

"I can only guess," Dray said. "From Saint Jeanne Military Prison to the Ministry of Justice is nearly sixteen kilometers. News sometimes travels very slowly in Burundi."

"It surprises me that Mboya should doubt your word about your whereabouts," Sandy said carefully, "from—when would it be?—I suppose the time you left us on the night before the attack until you were stopped at a checkpoint near Muramvya shortly before Hanson's murder."

"Why are you surprised, madame?" Dray smiled. "Mboya is paid to be skeptical."

"I am surprised because I assume that you told him the truth—whatever that might be."

63

"Telling the truth is sufficiently demanding that doing it once a day is usually as much as I can manage. I am so charmed by your approach to interrogation by indirection that I will nevertheless take one more stab at it, at least insofar as it implicates the point you mentioned. I returned to the campsite as arranged roughly twenty-four hours after I left you."

"And found Thomas and me missing."

"Correct. The campsite appeared to have been cleared in hasty but orderly fashion by more than two people. There was nothing valuable left, and it was apparent that the latrine had not been used since early morning. I was alarmed."

"Naturally. But not alarmed enough either to search for us or to return to Bujumbura?"

"With darkness approaching a search would have been futile," Dray explained. "Even if I had had any idea of where to look, which I did not. The obvious course was to drive to the nearest market town to try to find out what was going on. I headed for Muramvya. Ndala's men stopped me at a roadblock two kilometers short of the city. They let me cool my heels for about twelve hours while they verified my identity in rather leisurely fashion. Then they told me to proceed directly to Bujumbura, which I did."

"Thank you," Sandy said.

"It is nothing. I hope I have helped you, madame."

"You have been most kind. If you do not mind answering one more question?"

"Certainly."

"Is there someone at the French or Belgian embassies I might contact for more information about Kerry Travis?"

"Not the Belgian, certainly. It is all my poor compatriot diplomats can do to keep tabs on the Flems and Walloons running around Burundi, without worrying about Americans."

"The French Embassy, then?"

"If there is anyone there who can help you," Dray said, delicately picking his words, "contacting him would be the most certain way of shutting him up. But there is a reception scheduled there to celebrate Burundi's National Day. Such events conventionally represent an opportunity for unostentatious contacts between French diplomats and the real world. I will see if I can arrange for such a person to get in touch with you."

"That would be very gracious."

"Yes," Dray said. "I know it would."

Unscrewing the cap from the silver metal can, Thomas removed a round cassette of Tri-X Pan black-and-white thirty-five-millimeter film. A tongue of gray, perforated film, perhaps two inches long, stuck outside the cassette.

Thomas gripped the cassette spools between the thumb and index finger of his left hand, and the end of the film leader between the thumb and index finger of his right. Facing the late afternoon sun that streamed through his hotel room window, he raised the cassette to eye level and pulled the film smoothly out until his right arm was fully extended.

He let go of the raw film, now considerably overexposed. Opening the file blade from the nail clippers on his dresser, he inserted the point in the top of the cassette spool and started to turn it clockwise. The take-up spool moved easily. In less than ten seconds, the tip of the exposed film disappeared inside the cassette.

Picking up the phone, he asked to speak to the concierge. A simultaneously bored and impatient male voice came on the line two minutes later and demanded in French to know what Thomas wanted.

"For one hundred French francs," Thomas said in English, "I need a cab that can take me some place where I can get film developed very fast. Very fast film."

"Come down in ten minutes," the concierge said. In English.

13

"Do you think he was telling the truth?" Mboya asked Sandy as he gazed reflectively at the patterns cast on his office floor by the remnants of afternoon sun making their way through his window.

"About killing Hanson I am not certain. About much of the rest he was certainly lying."

"Truth or lies, there is little new in what he told you."

"I assumed as much," Sandy said.

"Well, as Monsieur Curry said to me in Muramvya," Mboya murmured, "thank you for trying."

"The pleasure was mine. I take it, however, that my usefulness has been exhausted."

"From my standpoint?" Mboya asked. "Or from Devereaux's?"

"Yours. So far as Devereaux is concerned, it depends."

"Depends on what?"

"On whether you are willing to share with me whatever facts cause you to doubt his guilt—if you actually have any such doubts. That is what he really hopes I will learn from you and disclose to him."

"*If* I have any such doubts?" Mboya protested. "I could easily secure Devereaux's conviction with the evidence I found in Muramvya alone. Yet the investigation continues. Surely that suggests that the doubts I have professed are genuine."

"It suggests that you think there is more to the killing than a panicky shot by a fugitive and that Devereaux therefore knows more than he is telling. You believe that Devereaux can be persuaded to trade this information for his life. You hoped to use me to verify this and to procure enough facts from Devereaux to make this transaction easier and faster for you. None of this is inconsistent with your being convinced that Devereaux in fact killed Hanson."

Rising from behind his desk, Mboya folded his hands behind his back and paced ponderously toward the window. His shoulder brushed a green silk, gold-fringed Kingdom of Burundi flag. As Sandy's explanation to Thomas shortly after they both met Mboya had implied, *juges d'instruction* are the conscience of the inquisitorial criminal justice system found in most of Europe and most former European colonies. For all practical purposes, they're the difference between justice and tyranny. When one of them who doesn't do his job right looks in the mirror, he ought to see Kafka's desiccated death's head looking back.

"You sound reproachful, Madame Curry," Mboya said.

"I do not mean to. I do not object particularly to Devereaux deceiving me or for that matter to you doing so. But I decline to deceive myself."

With startling abruptness Mboya whirled around to face Sandy.

"You said that I hoped to use you, and you were correct. I made no secret of my purposes. But I did not deceive you."

He strode back to the desk, opened the file on top of it, and pulled out three pages of flimsy onionskin. In a sharp, staccatto voice, he began rattling out facts that he read from the papers.

"After Bujumbura finally ordered Major Ndala to let me into the room where the body was found, I discovered the following: The body on the bed was that of a white male. It was naked, lying prone. Apparent cause of death, since confirmed, was a gunshot to the back of the head. Entrance wound consistent with a .45-caliber handgun bullet. Exit wound obliterated most of the face, suggesting use of expanding bullet. Absence of major bullet fragment tends to confirm. Impossible to estimate time of death because of delay in examining body. Gross, bluish purple discoloration at back of both shoulders and neck."

Pausing, he glanced for a moment at Sandy, his face unsmiling. Then he resumed his rapid-fire recitation from the report.

"Passport and residency permit discovered with body were those of Alex Hanson, identified as an American legally residing in Burundi since shortly before independence."

"And yet," Sandy said, "the guest registered to that room had turned over to the innkeeper an Irish passport issued to Terence Donoghue."

"An ostensible Irish passport," Mboya corrected her. "The Donoghue passport is fake. The Hanson passport is genuine."

"The inference does seem clear," Sandy said.

"Quite. Hanson wished to conceal his identity, so he turned a false passport over to the innkeeper and kept his own, genuine passport to himself."

"Please continue," Sandy invited Mboya, nodding at the report.

"Very well. Full set of dentures discovered on floor in damp area, near tumbler that had apparently fallen from bedside table. Report from Pasteur Clinic, Bujumbura, confirms that dentures match those fitted to Hanson there approximately four months ago. Fingerprints on tumbler, bed table, and door of wardrobe all match Hanson's fingerprints obtained from United States Army through U.S. Embassy."

"What about fingerprints taken from the body itself?"

"A question calling for a somewhat grisly answer, Madame Curry," Mboya nodded, smiling slightly. "Rigor mortis had set in by the time I obtained access to the body. Taking fingerprints after rigor mortis has set in requires a hot paraffin injection underneath the skin, for which there were no facilities in Muramvya. By the time the body had been returned to

68

Bujumbura, putrefaction was well advanced and fingerprinting was impossible."

" 'Grisly' is precisely the term for it," Sandy said.

"Examination of pillow underneath victim's head disclosed stains of what appeared to be dried blood and flesh, since confirmed as same, embedded grains of gunpowder, and fragments of lead."

"What is Major Ndala's explanation for not arresting Devereaux immediately after he came upon him following the ambush?" Sandy asked.

"He says that Devereaux was simply a name on a document to him. He denies ever seeing him before. He denies having or caring about any description of him. He points out rather acidly that he is a soldier rather than a policeman."

Sandy bobbed her head as Mboya again looked up at her.

"In short," she said, "the evidence is both tantalizing and abundant, but it leaves key questions unresolved."

"Being a *juge d'instruction* is my *profession,* Madame Curry."

"I understand," Sandy murmured.

"I am not certain that you do. Not entirely." Softening a bit, he put down the onionskin pages and took one step back from his desk. "A murder has been committed in my jurisdiction, and I care about that. I wish to get credit for clearing the matter up, for securing a conviction, and seeing appropriate punishment imposed. But most of all I care about *getting it right.* I do not have to be certain to hang Claude Devereaux. But I do have to be certain to satisfy myself."

Sandy received the implicit reprimand stoically, resisting the almost overpowering temptation to break eye contact with Mboya. She waited for two full seconds after his rolling cadences had stopped to be sure he was finished.

"I apologize if I offended you," she said. "I did not intend to. I wish you luck in your investigation, and I am sure you will let me know if I can be of further assistance to you in connection with this matter."

"I certainly shall," Mboya said. "And I hope you will let me know if Laurent Dray is of further assistance to you in the same connection."

14

"One hundred dollars American," the concierge said to Thomas and the cabbie after Thomas had climbed into an ancient, black Citroën taxi. The cabbie was a Hutu, a little taller than average.

"A hundred dollars?" Thomas yelped. "I could get the film custom-finished by George Eastman personally for that."

"Many mouths to feed on this type of thing," the concierge said, rolling his syllables in an affectation of what he took to be Gallic cynicism.

Through the window Thomas handed the concierge four twenties, a ten, and two fives. Even rich people didn't walk around with rolls of hundred dollar bills in 1963. After pocketing Thomas's money, the concierge gave a wad of Burundi bank notes to the cabbie, along with a short, sharp instruction in Kirundi.

The Citroën lurched away from the curb and began weaving through bicycles, handcarts, and occasional cars that shared streets with Hutu, Watusi, and a large enough number of Indian and Chinese pedestrians to surprise Thomas.

Thomas unfastened two buttons on his shirt, just above the waistband on his trousers. Leaving two twenty-dollar American Express checks and ten dollars worth of local currency in his wallet, he transferred the rest of his money, his driver's license, and all of his credit cards to the zipper pouch of a canvas money belt that he had strapped around his waist inside his shirt.

The cab climbed by fits and starts toward the high, cool, expensive part of Bujumbura. Teeming streets turned into nearly vacant avenues bordered by large houses that tall stone walls surrounded. Cars became less occasional. When he started seeing uniformed guards at the gates in the walls, Thomas realized that they were driving through the compact, particularly pricey Bujumbura real estate that included the western embassies' compound.

Turning right on a side street, they drove past a dozen shiny, angle-parked black cars with the flags of various countries on their fender posts. At the end of that long block, the cabbie turned right again and parked in the shade provided by a cedar tree.

Without taking his eyes off the windshield, the cabbie awkwardly stretched his right hand, palm up, over the back of the front seat toward Thomas.

"I think not," Thomas said in his barely passable French. "Let's take it together to wherever it's going."

The cabbie glanced over his shoulder, the whites of his eyes large as he raised his eyebrows in interrogation.

"I'm coming too," Thomas said. "Let's go."

He opened his door and started to get out. After a moment's indecision, the driver pulled himself from the cab as well.

Thomas followed the cabbie on foot back to the top of the block where the embassies' limousines were parked. They stopped there. After a moment of uncertain gazing toward the cars, the cabbie squatted on his haunches and began randomly to rearrange a handful of pebbles in the gutter. His white, open-necked shirt stretched tight across his perspiration-soaked upper back as he bent forward to gather the small stones. Thomas put his hands in his pockets and tried to look

71

as if he felt perfectly natural standing there without the faintest idea of what to do next.

Two long minutes passed. Then the driver's door on a limousine two-thirds of the way down the line of cars opened. A three-by-five-inch French tricolor fluttered on its fender post. A short black man in gray flannel trousers with a black bow tie at the neck of his white shirt got out and strolled toward them. The cabbie stood up as this man approached. They chatted with each other in Kirundi for the better part of a minute. Then the cabbie handed him some of the Burundi bank notes and jerked his head toward Thomas.

"How quickly can you get this taken care of?" Thomas asked the man from the embassy car in French.

The man spread his arms and offered Thomas an uncomprehending expression. Thomas repeated the question more slowly and with more elaborate pronunciation, nodding toward the French flag on the car the man had come from as he did so.

"Hour, could be," the man said.

"How are you going to get it done?"

"Lab in embassy, buddy on staff."

Thomas took the roll of film out of his pocket and started to hand it to the embassy driver. Instead of completing the transfer, however, he very nearly dropped it on the ground as the man suddenly and without the slightest warning executed a perfect about-face. With indecent haste he began retreating toward the limousine.

The cabbie shot startled glances to his left and right. Crossing the street toward them were two Watusi wearing European-cut sport coats and casual slacks. Confident eyes gazed out of their smooth, angular faces. Without hurrying, they moved steadily and unambiguously in Thomas's direction. Thomas looked behind him to confirm that another Tutsi had taken up a position in between the Citroën and Thomas. The first two stopped less than three feet from Thomas.

"Bone-jure," Thomas said, grinning like a Kiwanis Club president and achieving something close to a midwestern twang as he shamelessly exaggerated the amateurishness of his pronunciation. "Come on tally view?"

"Let's have it, slick," the taller of the two Watusi said in

72

English considerably better than Thomas's French. Bantu sibilants distorted only slightly the west Georgia accent that, Thomas surmised, was a legacy of Belgium's NATO membership. The Tutsi held out his left hand, palm up. With his right he swept his jacket back far enough to expose a Browning 9mm semiautomatic pistol.

Thomas tossed the man the film spool.

"Wear it in good health," he said.

The Tutsi looked at the cassette curiously for a moment before slipping it into his coat pocket. Then he thrust his hand out again.

"Wallet, too," he said.

"You don't really think you're kidding anyone, do you?" Thomas asked.

"You wastin' my time, boy." He snapped the large hand impatiently open and shut a couple of times.

Digging his slim billfold from his pocket, Thomas flipped it to the gunman, who caught it and dropped it into his pocket as well. Then the Tutsi abruptly slammed the back of his meaty hand against the Hutu cabbie's chest, accompanying the gesture with a harsh stream of Kirundi. Recovering after staggering backward for a moment, the cabbie handed a fistful of money to the Tutsi.

"Don't move for ten minutes," the Tutsi said.

He and his companion turned around and, everything in their manner suggesting utter confidence that he would be obeyed, walked jauntily away.

15

"How can you be certain they were soldiers rather than common thugs or policemen in plainclothes?" Sandy demanded.

Thomas studied a morsel of fork-speared chateaubriand for a moment, admiring the highlights that the silverware picked up from the flickering candle at their table in the Hotel Spaak's dining room.

"Jump boots," he said then.

"They were wearing paratroop boots?"

"Yes. Every detective story I've ever read says that people disguising their dress change everything but their footwear. So the jump boots are one. Two is, the pistol he showed me was a Belgian make, and I'm about 90 percent sure that model is the standard officer's side arm in the Burundi Army. Three, the one who talked had spent some time with American soldiers and for someone in a Belgain trust territory that means he's a lot more likely to be a soldier than a cop."

Sandy washed some cheese crêpe down with a generous swallow of white wine.

"Your argument does not lack force," she conceded.

"Thank you."

"But it is not conclusive. Your evidence suggests that these men were Burundi soldiers at one time—not necessarily now. It would not be surprising for the Bujumbura *police judiciaire* to include many veterans of the Burundi armed forces."

"Three veterans who all changed their careers recently enough that they hadn't worn out their last pair of army boots all draw the same assignment?" Thomas asked skeptically. "A bit of a reach, isn't it?"

"Perhaps," Sandy said.

"Besides, you've given Mboya the real film. If it turned out to be salvageable, he's had a chance to get it developed and verify that it consists of pictures of sunrise from a vantage point near the attack, which is what the real film is supposed to have. Unlike the major, he doesn't have any reason to be interested in any other film that we have."

"But you are begging the question," Sandy said. "You are assuming that the major is interested, and then using that assumption to prove that he took what you say he was interested in."

"It's not an assumption. He confiscated our camera and what he thought was the film that'd been in it. He's had plenty of time to get the film you gave him developed and see that the last pictures on it are of elephants. Presumably, he knows that the nearest elephant migration route is a considerable distance from the vicinity of the attack. Hence, he knows what you gave him couldn't be film from the morning of the attack, and he'd logically assume that we still had that film." Thomas paused for a moment before adding, Sandy-like, "Q.E.D."

"Do I sound that dogmatic when I do one of my Q.E.D.s?" she asked.

"No. You sound perfectly charming."

"I believe you are patronizing me."

"Sandy, you're being rather difficult to please."

Sandy glanced down at her plate. She closed her eyes. Her brown cheeks turned copperish near her ears. She laid down her knife and fork. She looked up and fixed Thomas with an icily penetrating royal blue gaze.

"You are right," she said. Her tone suggested that being

right was a capital offense. "My behavior has been rather petulant since we talked to Devereaux. I apologize. I seem to have done a lot of apologizing today."

"Please, Sandy, there's—"

"The reason for my ill temper is my conviction that it is needlessly and unproductively dangerous for you to be involved in this affair. I believe I expressed myself on that point this afternoon."

"I believe you did, at that," Thomas said.

"You have a past that I do not share."

"And you have a present that I do share."

"Clever rhetoric, empty argument," Sandy said. "I am trying to do the same thing you did when you threw me on the ground during the attack to keep me from catching a bullet because of my impetuous imprudence."

"I know that."

"Then why do you refuse to cooperate?"

"Why did you object when I threw you down?"

"Ignorance," Sandy said. "An excuse you do not have. My ignorance was quickly remedied. Your stubbornness is proving less tractable."

"Sandy," Thomas said with a suggestion of finality, "I am not going to sit idly by while you conceal evidence from soldiers and interview condemned men and confront investigating magistrates. If that's the game—fine. No complaints. But I'm part of it. When you involve yourself, you involve me."

"Translation: You are too proud to accept my protection."

"If you like," Thomas shrugged.

"But you expect me to accept yours."

"I want you to accept my help. Because you're going to get it whether you like it or not."

Instead of losing her temper at this provocative, I-have-spoken decree, Sandy willed herself to a steely self-control. She settled back in her chair. She raised her wine glass and took a deliberate sip, savoring the dry liquid on her tongue before swallowing it. She set the glass delicately back down. She folded her arms across her chest, under her breasts.

"I sense that I haven't won you over entirely to my position," Thomas said.

"I do not wish to discuss the matter any further."

"Fine. Would you care to introduce another topic?"

"*Je crois que non.*"

"The burden falls on me," Thomas sighed. "Might as well start with Dray. Do you really think he can deliver on his promise to find someone who'll tell you about—"

Thomas interrupted his own question because the maitre d' had just appeared at his elbow with a salver holding a thick, cream-colored, invitation-size envelope. It was addressed to Mr. and Mrs. Thomas Curry. Thomas took it from the salver, opened it along the top, and read to Sandy the handwritten, almost calligraphic note inside.

" 'His Excellency Maurice Badinter, Ambassador of France to the Kingdom of Burundi, requests the honor of the presence of Monsieur Thomas Andrew Curry and Madame Sandrine Cadette Curry at a midnight supper and reception in celebration of Burundi's National Sovereignty Day beginning at 2330 hours, 9 July 1963.' Well, that answers that question. Dray must have procured this for us, right?"

"Nine July?" Sandy gasped. "That is tonight." She glanced at her watch. "It is nearly 8:00 P.M. already. Please ask for the check at once."

"Yes," Thomas said as he obediently gestured toward the waiter. "I thought he had."

16

The desk clerk at the Hotel Lesotho in Leopoldville handed me Thomas's message sometime between 9:30 and 9:45 that night, when I returned from a long and expensive dinner with the senior deputy to the Congolese minister of public works. The typewritten note said that Thomas's call had come in over an hour before. The message itself was short and to the point: "Theodore, I need your help. TAC."

How many times had I left a message like that for Thomas? How many times had I pulled him into the office at night or on weekends to provide the special, unlicensed but effective legal services that his free-lance relationship with me made possible? How many times had he dropped everything and come in without question to earn a small amount of money that he didn't need, without any explanation beyond the flat assertion that I needed his help?

Too many times for there to be any question of how I'd respond to the same plea from him.

I went to the concierge's desk and tinkled the black-handled, brass-cupped miniature school bell resting there. A tall man with the marbled features, bristling hair, and I've-seen-things-you-haven't-seen gleam in his eye that I've always associated with white Russian émigrés emerged from a small door behind the desk, struggling into his uniform jacket as he did so.

"What are the chances of getting a flight to Bujumbura yet tonight?" I asked in impeccable French.

"Zero," he said in English.

"When's the first flight tomorrow morning?"

"Eight A.M.," he said. "If the airport is open."

"Why shouldn't the airport be open?"

"Trouble in the countryside."

"That's nothing unusual," I said.

"More trouble than usual. Much more. A constabulary near the eastern border has been overrun, convents and clinics being burned, nuns being raped—it's 1962 all over again north of Katanga Province."

"That's all a long way from Leopoldville. That kind of thing can't be threatening the airport here."

"Not yet," the concierge conceded. "But *Agence France Press* is filing lurid dispatches. European opinion and the UN command are getting nervous at the same time. There are rumors that the airport may be preempted for Belgian marines and Congolese paratroops."

I shuddered inside. Remember what the Duke of Wellington said about the British Army—he didn't know if it scared the French, but it certainly frightened the devil out of him? That's the way I felt about Congolese paratroops. I would've preferred for them to be flying into Stanleyville or Elizabethville or someplace else closer to Katanga and several hundred miles from me.

"Please get me a ticket on the first flight tomorrow morning, open return," I said.

"And if the airport is closed?"

"I'm an optimist. But just in case, arrange for a car and a driver. We'll see if the airport's open in Brazzaville, and if that doesn't work we'll set off cross-country."

"Did I mention nuns being raped and constabularies being burned? I doubt that you will find any drivers willing to risk an overland trip all the way across the Congo to Burundi."

"That means if you find one things will have quieted down enough that I'll have nothing to worry about," I said.

"You are an optimist. As you wish, Monsieur Furst."

Leaving him a somewhat more modest tip than he would've gotten if he'd answered me in French, I went upstairs to phone my client, read a couple of dozen pages in *The Guns of August,* and wished fervently that I believed what I'd just said to the concierge.

17

"You are dazzling this evening, Madame Curry," Dray said.

"Thank you very much," Sandy said. "And thank you for arranging this invitation on such short notice."

"*Il n'y a pas de quoi.*" Dray nibbled on a postage-stamp-size piece of truffle. "Where is Monsieur Curry?"

"Mingling. Somewhere," Sandy said.

"The gentleman standing underneath that atrocity by David in the corner is a cultural affairs attaché here. His name is Lionel Bettati. I have it on good authority that he is anxious to make your acquaintance."

"Perhaps someone will introduce us," Sandy said.

"I think you can count on him not to stand on ceremony," Dray said.

"Is he anxious to talk about Kerry Travis?"

"He is anxious to learn about Claude Devereaux. If Monsieur Travis's name should come up in the course of a chat on that topic, I am sure that Bettati will be able to hold up his end of the conversation."

"Thank you again," Sandy said.

Dray smiled and shrugged. The silk facing on the lapel of his tuxedo jacket brushed Sandy's bare shoulder lightly as he moved away.

Vertical cream-colored stripes periodically broke the matte red, gold-trimmed finish on the wall in the French Embassy's immense reception salon. Blue and amber highlights flashed in the facets of the crystal chandelier that glittered above an abundant buffet laid out on two long, intersecting tables. Massive canvases by Delacroix, Ingres, Gerard, Denon, and the David atrocity mentioned by Dray decorated the walls at tasteful intervals. A string quartet at the north end of the room played selections from Berlioz and Debussy quietly enough not to interfere with the conversation. Mahogany chairs and sandalwood settees, looking as if they were meant more to be admired than sat in, took up the spaces in between the paintings.

The entire European and American communities in Bujumbura, together with most of Burundi's Watusi elite, had turned out in evening clothes and dress uniforms to toast the country's year-old independence. Their highly buffed shoes scraped the veined marble floor as they sampled the plentiful European food, brandy, and champagne.

The effect, Thomas thought, was almost disorienting. With the possible exceptions of the powerful air conditioning and the Kingdom of Burundi flag hanging next to the tricolor, nothing in the room—including the numerous black faces—evoked Africa in any distinctive way. Without changing a detail, it seemed to him that the scene might have been transported to Vienna or Lisbon, Washington or Rio de Janeiro, Bangkok or Kuala Lumpur, as if it were 1895 again and Europe still ruled an empire of timeless splendor.

Thomas assured me afterward that he had ignored no less than three anti-American gibes from the youthful French political affairs intern before he finally reacted. French diplomats, of course, like diplomats generally, are seldom rude except to people from their own country. This young man, however, wasn't a diplomat.

He was a twenty-year-old student at *L'Ecole Nationale d'Administration* whose already healthy ego had been reinforced when that school had selected him to be one of the handful of future *fonctionnaires* to spend a year at embassies, ministries, and other seats of the power they expected to be exercising soon. The French call these kids "Enarchs," and they aren't joking.

On top of that, this particular juvenile—Thomas didn't bother to remember his name, except that it was one of the double-d varieties indicating aristocratic lineage on both sides—was flushed with pride at the recent flowering of French grandeur and muscular independence under De-Gaulle's Fifth Republic. All things considered, a little swaggering might have been tolerated. Whatever limited tolerance Thomas had, however, had run out after the third crack, which involved a less than complimentary assessment of the way President Kennedy had handled the Laotian crisis the previous year.

Apparently sensing that things were about to get out of hand, the wife of the Italian commercial attaché intervened.

"Aren't the strings lovely?" she asked in English.

"Yes," Thomas said. "I wouldn't have minded hearing more of them, particularly during—"

"Indeed," the woman agreed hastily, forestalling a comparison of the relative merits of the strings and the French intern's comments. "After all, 'If music is the food of love, then 'tis folly to be thin.' Who said that?"

"No one," the wannabe diplomat assured her. "Until just now."

"Surely you are mistaken," she insisted. Then turning to Thomas she demanded, "Didn't Shakespeare say that?"

"I'm not certain that *William* Shakespeare said it," Thomas allowed judiciously. "But Sam Shakespeare may have. At any rate, I'm certain that he would have if he'd thought of it."

"Very droll," the Frenchman allowed as the Italian woman beamed.

"How do you come to be in Bujumbura?" she asked Thomas.

"A colleague of my wife's named Theodore Furst is in

Leopoldville trying to direct a government contract into nontraditional channels—French channels, as a matter of fact. Sandy and I decided to take a few days off and we came here."

Thomas has asked that the record show that up to this point he hadn't actually responded in kind to any of the young intern's remarks. He has solemnly insisted, in fact, that it was only when the kid directed his condescending attitude at me that Thomas was provoked beyond restraint. You can believe that if you want to.

"Your colleague has assumed a task disproportionate to his capabilities," the Frenchman said. "The paths of commercial intercourse with the Congo run to Brussels, not Paris or Lyon."

"That is precisely what makes the desired channels nontraditional," Thomas answered pleasantly.

"Old habits die hard."

"Furst is counting on the times being propitious for developing new habits."

"He will be disappointed," the intern asserted at that point, with the dogmatic confidence you never feel again after you're past your early twenties. "Colonials change flags, but they do not change mentalities. Ten years after France has recognized the independence of Morocco, Mali, and so forth, the native ruling classes will still smoke Gauloises. They'll still drink Dom Perignon. They'll still read Verlaine and *Le Monde*. And they'll still strut around in tricolor sashes at the slightest opportunity. The only thing different will be the colors on the sashes."

"Perhaps," Thomas shrugged in a halfhearted stab at a diplomatic response. "Furst thinks otherwise, and he's right more often than he's wrong."

"Then he is naïve." The young man finished his scotch and soda in a gulp. "Americans reflect the naïveté of innocence. Without exception."

"Frenchmen, on the other hand," Thomas smilingly rejoined, "reflect the finesse of experience—with some exceptions."

"A curious comment from someone whose government's policies have not suggested a particle of finesse in living memory."

"You have to be patient with us," Thomas yawned. "We're still on our first republic."

"Inasmuch as Monsieur Devereaux is a French national, his circumstances are naturally a concern to my government," Bettati was saying about ten minutes later to Sandy.

Sandy brusquely checked the flash of impatience that was about to slip across her face. After more than five minutes of chat, it seemed to Sandy that Bettati had yet to get past the delicate verbal waltz stage. If patience were worth a thousand dollars an ounce, Sandy could just about afford a cup of coffee. She decided to cut to the chase.

"Of two things, one must be true," she said in the clipped, Cartesian style universally taught at French *lycées* of her era. "One: Devereaux is guilty. In that case, he necessarily knows the information that may possibly save his life. The decision about using that information is his. Nothing further can be done to help him."

"And two?" Bettati prompted.

"Two: Devereaux is innocent. In that case, he may still know critical information, but what he knows need not be complete enough to interest Mboya."

"And so?"

"So any possibility of helping him necessarily involves Kerry Travis."

"How can one be certain that Travis had any meaningful involvement in any part of the affair?" Bettati demanded.

"One cannot. But one can be certain that Mboya thinks he does. Until that possibility is thoroughly explored, matters are *de facto* at an impasse, and the only interesting question is how long it will take Mboya to lose patience."

"And hang Devereaux."

"Or use the threat of hanging him to shake whatever information he has out of him, however marginal it is," Sandy said.

Bettati thought about that for a long moment before responding.

"Kerry Travis is not someone who goes out of his way to make his whereabouts known to authorities," Bettati said. "He is an American version of Devereaux, really. He came to the Congo over a year ago as a member of the Peace Corps. Within three months he had been 'selected out,' as the deplorable American bureaucratic jargon has it. The Americans are understandably a bit closemouthed about it, but the rumor is that he was deeply involved in smuggling."

"Smuggling what?"

"Whatever someone would pay him to smuggle."

"Then why would he come to a country that has less to smuggle than any other in central Africa?"

"The obvious answer is that he wanted to exploit the one thing that Burundi has in abundance."

"Coffee?" Sandy asked, feeling a bit stupid.

"Poverty," Bettati said.

Sandy considered the enigmatic comment for a moment.

"In a poor country," she said, "things can be bought cheap. And so can people."

"Yes. Particularly people who work for the government."

"Is there proof of this?"

"Six or seven months ago," Bettati said, "the Katangan rebels were supposedly rooted out of the Congo. They'd been defeated any time they'd been brought to battle."

"Yes," Sandy said. "The American news accounts said that Katangan resistance unexpectedly collapsed in early January."

"Exact," Bettati said. "When organized, armed resistance unexpectedly collapses, one cannot help wondering if those resisting have not been crushed but have simply melted away to fight another day."

"Is that what happened in Katanga?"

"*Evidemment*, according to tonight's reports," Bettati shrugged. "In the Congo, they could be systematically hunted down in the bush. Had they stayed there, they should have been either disarmed or wiped out."

"But perhaps they went somewhere else?"

"Well, there is always Rhodesia, for one example," Bettati said.

"And Burundi for another?"

"And Burundi."

"*D'accord*," Sandy said. "Monsieur Dray told us as much

86

the day before the attack on the convoy. But I thought at the time he was merely being melodramatic."

"Monsieur Dray is well informed. But the Burundi sanctuaries are no particular secret in Bujumbura."

"What links Travis to sanctuaries?" Sandy demanded.

"Inference."

"Inference from what data?"

"Monsieur Travis has been engaged in profitable activities that would be possible only with the active cooperation of armed elements in both the Congo and Burundi. We must assume that he has provided those elements with something valuable in exchange for their cooperation. Serving as an intermediary in transactions in which Katangan rebels get sanctuary and Burundi officers get money would qualify. It is not easy to think of anything else that would."

"Q.E.D.," Sandy said.

"*Evidemment.*" Bettati glanced sharply to his right as a strident and rising verbal tone from elsewhere in the room reached his trained ear. "If you will excuse me, madame, it appears that a modest bit of diplomacy may be called for near the buffet."

Sandy followed Bettati's gaze. She saw a small but animated group standing next to the caviar. Its most animated member was, if not exactly talking to Thomas, at least declaiming in his general direction. A number of people—an uncomfortably large number of people, from Sandy's standpoint—were watching. Trailing in Bettati's wake, Sandy with growing misgivings moved toward the verbal fracas.

"—implacable American will to hegemony," the intern was saying. "France is entitled to its own distinction, its own dimension—"

"Now, now," Bettati said jovially as he came up, "we must remember that this is a celebration of our host country's nationhood. What is this will to hegemony?"

"As nearly as I can tell," Thomas said, laying on the smart-aleck fraternity boy tone with a trowel, "it's either a contingent principle from Nietzche or the Red Sox 1943 double-play combination."

"Thomas, please," Sandy murmured.

"Puppy," the intern muttered disgustedly.

"Surely the culture that produced *Cyrano* can do better than that," Thomas scoffed. "You could call me a pettifogging shyster, for example. Or a pox-ridden pederast. Or an illegitimate product of an imperfectly consummated union between a clumsy dwarf and a careless streetwalker. Or even—" Thomas paused, enjoying the expectant silence that surrounded him. "Or even an undergraduate buffoon."

"Of course," the intern said, his lips snapping under flushed cheeks. "Everything is a joke. Everything is superficial. But France's place in the world is not a joke. And the United States will be made to understand that France's pursuit of its military and diplomatic independence will not be superficial."

"It would be interesting to see how independent French diplomacy would be if there weren't two hundred forty thousand Yanks standing in between Paris and the Red Army," Thomas said in the same flippant tone.

Bettati paled slightly. An undertone of commentary ran through the surrounding group. Sandy closed her eyes.

"That goes beyond repartee," the intern said. "That comment implicates my country's honor."

"Well, if you want pistols at sunrise the answer's no. I sleep late. Besides, I don't have time for it. I still have to talk to someone at this party about some film."

The young man flipped his right hand toward Thomas's face. A few driblets of melted ice cube arced inconsequentially onto the shoulders of Thomas's dinner jacket.

"That gesture is generally more effective if it's done before the glass's contents have been consumed," Thomas said.

Bettati reached for the man's arm. Sandy didn't wait for him to speak.

"Thank you for a stimulating and enjoyable evening, Monsieur Bettati," she said. "Thomas, please take me back to the hotel."

She turned and swept toward the door.

18

"I know you're upset," Thomas said, "but—"

"I am not upset," Sandy snapped over her shoulder as she quickstepped down the corridor ahead of him toward their suite at the Hotel Spaak.

"I thought I showed remarkable restraint, actually." Without making a production out of it, he quickened his pace to catch up to Sandy and then move slightly ahead of her. "I put up with his comments for quite a while."

Unlocking the door to their room, Thomas pushed it open, snapped on a light just inside the doorway, and peered inside for several seconds before he stepped aside to let Sandy enter. Sandy's efforts to conceal her impatience during this performance were less than heroic.

"If you had put up with his comments for ten minutes longer," she said crossly as she whipped into the room, brusquely and painfully detaching gold earrings as she went, "you would have avoided embarrassing our host."

"I apologize for any embarrassment—"

"You didn't embarrass *me,* so apologizing to me serves no purpose."

"I thought it might placate you to the extent of permitting me to complete two consecutive sentences. And if it wasn't you I embarrassed, why are you the one that's so angry?"

"I am *not* angry."

Sandy flung her earrings on top of the dresser, where they skidded across the waxed surface and rattled against the wall behind it.

"Why do you keep saying you're not angry when you're unarguably furious? Do women enjoy some dispensation from the Eighth Commandment for purposes of spousal argument?"

"Perhaps we could save theological disputation for a more appropriate occasion," Sandy said.

"Perhaps we could, at that. Listen, please. I thought I had every right to answer that pubescent windbag—"

"Of course you had every right to do so. I have every right to eat popcorn for breakfast. The fact that you have a right to do something does not necessarily make it a sensible thing to do."

"Fair enough," Thomas conceded. "If I did overstep the bounds of good judgment, that reflected an excess of zeal rather than churlishness or ill temper."

"An embassy reception is seldom the most promising forum for zealotry. Particularly a reception where I am seeking to gather information on a cooperative basis. I would have preferred less zeal and more tact."

"I don't claim to be a diplomat."

"You do claim to be an adult."

"Only because I have no choice."

"So I have noticed. Besides," Sandy said as she ungently delivered black patent leather high-heeled shoes seriatim to the floor, "neither zeal nor ill temper explains that last remark you made about film. That was calculated intermeddling."

"Oh," Thomas said. "You noticed that."

"Of course I noticed it. I also noticed your inspection of the room before you let me in. I know exactly what you are up to. You have been trying to attract attention to yourself in a self-appointed effort to divert it from me."

"I did give you fair warning."

"That is not a mitigating circumstance but an aggravating

one. It shows premeditation." Sandy had by now left her remaining clothes in a heap on the floor and stepped into a bathrobe. Thomas winced as she cinched the sash tightly around her waist.

"You'd do exactly the same thing if our positions were reversed."

"You are presumptuous. That is in addition to being meddlesome, exasperating, and infuriating."

"Thank heaven I'm not ill-bred," Thomas sighed.

"Your skill at repartee has already been amply displayed this evening," Sandy said. "But cleverness is no excuse for childishness. If I outweighed you by sixty pounds instead of the other way around, you would eat your next meal standing up."

Turning her back on Thomas, Sandy hurtled into the bathroom and slammed the door. The immediate sound of running water precluded any possibility of continuing the conversation.

A tired half smile accompanying his shrug, Thomas loosened his black silk bow tie and unfastened the top button of his shirt.

"When will I learn?" he asked as he paced unhurriedly around the small room. "Of course, I'm probably not the first husband to have that question occur to him."

A sliver of white silk negligee had been peeking above the lip of a lower dresser drawer when they had left. It no longer showed when they returned. Thomas suspected rather strongly that Sandy had noticed. She hadn't mentioned it to him. Of course, he hadn't mentioned it to her, either. Probably for the same reason.

Thomas wrote "Going for a walk" on a piece of hotel stationery that he wedged into the top of Sandy's purse. As he did so he noticed her cigarette case. A quick, instinctive check established that the case was empty.

Thomas shook two Winstons from the case inside his jacket and left them beside Sandy's purse. Childishness is no excuse for thoughtlessness—or for stupidity.

19

Never tell the truth during an argument with your wife.

This proposition seemed to Thomas to combine the deep resonance of eternal truth with the intuitive certainty of searing insight. How it could have gone unremarked over the centuries was a mystery, upon which Thomas reflected with philosophic resignation as he watched the Hotel Spaak's moonlit outline and listened to Lake Tanganyika lapping gently against the concrete mooring wall behind him.

Things had been going reasonably well, actually, as long as he limited himself to nuanced contrition and boyish flippancy. Sandy was getting it out of her system, her passionate fury gradually giving way to simple anger as their fight proceeded along a predictable parabola toward cathartic resolution.

Then he'd made the mistake of telling her the truth. *You'd have done exactly the same thing if our situations had been reversed.* Brilliant. True. Unanswerable. Infuriating.

Oh well. Live and learn. He puffed briefly on his cigar and walked a few steps along the lakefront behind the hotel.

Thinking about the fight with Sandy was unproductive. Also depressing. He decided to think about something else.

Why had Devereaux gotten Sandy involved in the Muramvya murder investigation? This question puzzled Thomas. With a flash of pleasure, he imagined Sandy analyzing it in a series of lancing, Cartesian propositions.

Devereaux had at least two possible reasons for involving Sandy. One: to keep Mboya honest. Two: to extract information from Mboya and relay it to Devereaux.

How much sense did the first possibility make? If Devereaux were guilty, then the more thoroughly Mboya did his job the more completely Devereaux's guilt would be established. So the first possibility worked only if Devereaux were innocent.

Okay, consider the second possibility. Why would Devereaux want information about how Mboya's investigation was going? So that he could use that data to decide what he was going to tell Mboya and when he was going to tell it.

This made sense only if there were something Devereaux hadn't yet told Mboya. If Devereaux were guilty, then every hour's delay in spilling his guts to Mboya increased the risk that Mboya would learn independently whatever Devereaux had to tell, which would make Devereaux's own information worthless. So why would Devereaux delay disclosing what he knew to Mboya? Because there was some disadvantage to disclosure which outweighed that risk.

Like what? Like exposing Devereaux to prosecution for some other crime that he had to have been involved in in order to know what he knew. Or like getting himself killed by whoever the real murderer in Muramvya had been. Or both.

How did involving Sandy solve these problems? By making it possible for Devereaux to channel critical information to Mboya without compromising himself. Which would work only if disclosing that information would exculpate Devereaux. Otherwise, he'd accomplish nothing but to destroy any possibility of trading what he knew for lenient treatment from Mboya.

"That's interesting," Thomas said in a conversational tone to the shadows surrounding him. "Devereaux's action doesn't make sense on any hypothesis unless he's innocent. But how could he possibly be innocent?''

Thomas stared into the inky blackness extending to the hotel building forty feet away. He brushed aside the flaring intuition that people were waiting there, watching him from the darkness. Ndala knew by now that the film his men had taken from Thomas that afternoon was fake. But he'd had the hotel room searched while Thomas and Sandy were at the embassy reception, so he knew there wasn't any film there—ought to know that there wasn't any film period, except what Sandy had long since turned over to Mboya. If he'd gotten wind of Thomas's provocative lie about film at the French Embassy reception, he'd presumably picked up the implication of Thomas's comment, which was that someone at the embassy already had the imaginary stuff.

So, Thomas reasoned confidently: No reason for Ndala to bother further with him—or, more important, with Sandy. Yet, for another solid minute he stood still, gazing reflectively at the night, instincts from what seemed another life pulsing through his nerves and muscles.

It all seemed so long ago. Before he was a bachelor of arts, before he was a bachelor of legal law, before he was an assistant United States attorney, before he was a former attorney. Korea and then Algeria. The adrenaline surge when you saw yellow-orange and blue-white flashes from the guns below, the thrilling conviction of indestructibility when you brought your copter through them in one piece. He'd gone to Korea to show his father that money wasn't enough to push him around. He said he'd gone to Algeria for the same reason, but he realized now there'd been more to it than that. He'd wanted to feel it some more.

Mboya was smart and Sandy was Sandy, but Thomas knew he brought something to this enterprise that neither of them did. Thomas understood Claude Devereaux in a way that Sandy and Mboya couldn't. And he understood Major Ndala.

Thomas took a couple of strides toward the stone steps that led up from the dock to the Hotel Spaak's patio, casually removing his dinner jacket and slinging it over his shoulder as he did so. The weight of his tobacco case in the jacket's inside pocket seemed vaguely reassuring as it nestled against his right shoulder blade. He paused, halfway expecting attackers to show their hand, ready when they did to quickstep back to the mooring wall, jump into the lake, and swim for it. If they were there at all, he was confident that was a maneuver they wouldn't be prepared for.

Thomas wasn't sure what giveaway he expected—shuffling combat boots, a muffled shout or two—but whatever it was he didn't hear it. A sheepish sense of anticlimax building in him, he continued onto the flagstones, paused again, heard nothing again. Wariness dissipating by the second, he strolled at an increasingly relaxed pace until he was more than twenty-five yards from the dock.

That's when he heard it.

Sole leather scraped about twenty feet ahead of him. He glanced in that direction in time to see two shapes detach themselves from the darkness near the hotel and move toward him. They weren't being shy about it.

It took only a hurried glance to spot menacing strangers moving along the lakefront to his right, behind the hotel, and to his left. If he retreated now, either group could intercept him before he reached the dock. That left him with one option.

Thomas attacked. He ran straight at the two men between him and the hotel. Bunching his jacket in both hands near his chest, he threw it a yard before contact at the head of the nearer man, like a two-hand set-shot left over from the 1948 NIT. It hit the man's face with a dull splat as Thomas lowered his head and at full speed butted the second man in the hollow diamond between his lungs and his belt. Literally breathless for a moment after air exploded from his body, the man collapsed like a cheap tent in a hurricane.

Scrambling from on top of his victim, Thomas chanced a hasty look at the other attacker. Mistake. Deterred for only a moment by the jacket, the man lashed out with a long-legged snap-kick. Even the glancing heel blow that Thomas caught near his temple when he ducked away sent him staggering off balance and nearly stunned him.

Awkwardly recovering his stance, Thomas sprinted for the hotel's protective shadow. Hustling steps slapped the flagstones behind him.

The number of millionaires who can outrun paratroops

isn't large, and Thomas didn't think he was one of them. He tried desperately to recall what the patio and the area beyond it looked like. A vague mental image of a receiving dock forced its way to the top of his mind.

He definitely didn't remember the low brick wall just past the patio tables. Stumbling over that cost him a second and a couple of scrapes, but a moment or two after he resumed his run he heard a thud and a curse behind him suggesting that his nearest pursuer had also acquainted himself unexpectedly with the barrier.

Panting along next to the hotel wall as the footing changed from flagstones to clay, completely shielded from the moonlight, Thomas was invisible to the men closing in from the lakefront. Thomas had only a dozen feet or so on the man chasing him, but if the dock would just come up here somewhere, that twelve feet might be enough.

His increasingly panicked feet smacked against asphalt. Thomas looked up. The receiving dock loomed on his left. Almost without breaking stride, Thomas pressed two grateful hands on top of it and vaulted onto the platform.

A confused hissing of whispers and gasps greeted him. For an instant he thought he'd jumped straight into an ambush. But no challenge or contact followed the noise. He couldn't even see where it had come from or who had caused it.

The man chasing him was shouting something to his closest companions, but it shouldn't make any difference now. Thomas found the massive double door in the near back corner of the dock and pounded on it. Pushing four o'clock in the morning, less than an hour and a half to daylight, there had to be someone back there ready to receive the day's supply of fish and vegetables that would be coming soon.

It was a great theory, but mocking echoes of his blows were all that answered him. Thomas looked around in time to see his pursuer and at least one reinforcement pull themselves onto the dock.

Fresh out of bright ideas, Thomas turned to face his attackers. After feinting in one direction, he dove with his fists into the tall soldier who was almost on top of him. He landed three solid punches on the man's ribs before a massive, shattering two-punch combination to his face sent his head snapping violently back against the metal and cinder block. He felt only an instant's pain before he plunged into deep unconsciousness.

20

I finally saw Thomas not quite eleven hours later, around two-thirty that afternoon. Actually, I saw part of him. Past the white linen wimple and pale blue, floor-length robe of a Vincentian nun, I glimpsed Thomas's heavily bandaged head and bruised, blue-and-yellow face.

I was trying to get to where I could see more, but the nun had other ideas. I'm a little embarrassed about not being able to get past her but all I can say is, you try it sometime. My efforts had transcended importunate and were rapidly approaching obnoxious when a white-coated physician hurried over to reinforce the nun.

"Monsieur Curry cannot possibly be disturbed," the doctor said with that authoritarian dogmatism that's passed for bedside manner with French physicians since the Napoleonic Wars. "He is lucky to be alive."

"What happened to him?" I asked.

"He apparently had the worst of a fight with at least two Watusi," the doctor said. "The men who brought him in said that there were five Watusi, but I discount that by up to 60 percent."

I took this with even less composure than you might expect. The 8:10 A.M. flight from Leopoldville to Bujumbura had taken off promptly at 10:45 A.M. I'd spent the morning leaving messages for Thomas and Sandy at their hotel. The last message had mentioned my ETA, but there wasn't any word from them waiting for me at the airport when I finally got to Bujumbura, sometime between 1:30 and 2:00.

After a harrowing cab ride through drizzling rain to the Hotel Spaak, the news had gotten worse. What I found there was a note from Sandy saying that Thomas was at Saint Vincent de Paul Hospital and asking me to deliver an attached envelope to him. As he handed me the envelope, the chatty desk clerk leeringly mentioned that Monsieur and Madame Coo-*rie* had had an argument last night that was loud and spirited enough to have become the talk of the entire staff.

It was with pronounced misgivings, to put it mildly, that I got the doctor's version of what had landed Thomas in a hospital bed. The implacable refusal to let me try for a coherent explanation from Thomas didn't help at all.

I used every ounce of my considerable charm on the doctor. When that got me nowhere, I tried an approach that stopped just short of making *The Ugly American* look like non-fiction.

The physician wasn't impressed.

"He is under sedation," he said. "Check back in perhaps two hours. No promises."

End of discussion.

The cab I had taken from the hotel wasn't waiting for me outside. The rain was. Feeling useless and frustrated and nourishing a vague hope of waiting out the rain, I slumped in a straw-bottomed chair in the hospital lobby while I thought about what to do next.

I want you to know that I really had to struggle with my conscience before I could bring myself to open the envelope that Sandy had asked me to take to Thomas. My conscience put up a good fight. Like Thomas, though, it ended up with nothing but swollen knuckles to show for the effort.

Inside the envelope was a note written in Sandy's unmistakable longhand on pale green, quadrille-lined lab-report paper, which was what Sandy wrote anything on if she had the

99

choice. Its few short words left my stomach feeling icy and my throat tight:

> Thomas—*Dommage*. Together we could have handled them. I must leave, and you must stay. I know you will understand. This is the best way. *Actio fidei.*

Actio Fidei. Act of faith. A term of chilling implication for an educated Catholic with a mordant sense of humor. "Act of Faith" was what the Inquisition called the elaborately choreographed immolation of heretics and their works at the stake— the fiery destruction of something pernicious, based on the hard, uncompromising premise that error has no rights.

That was when I noticed the polite, young black man standing about thirty inches from me. After verifying that I was the American named Theodore Furst who had left a message for the Currys at the Hotel Spaak that morning and cleared customs in Bujumbura after arriving from Leopoldville that afternoon, he informed me that *Juge d'instruction* Mboya would be very pleased if I could come to the *Palais de Justice* for a chat with him. Immediately. I was *not* under arrest. For some reason, the young man thought it important to be very clear on that point.

"How much do you know about what happened to your friend?" Mboya asked after scampering through the standard preliminaries.

"The attending physician told me that he got into a fight with some, uh, Burundians," I said. I didn't want to say "natives" like some misplaced refugee from the British Raj, and I thought it might be impolitic in a conversation with a Tutsi official to describe Thomas's antagonists as Watusi.

"It is somewhat more complicated than that," Mboya said.

"In what way?"

"Monsieur Curry was apparently attacked by Watusi soldiers in civilian clothes after he and Madame Curry had returned to their hotel following a midnight reception at the French Embassy. He was beaten senseless. Fortunately for him, he managed in the process to stumble into a group of

100

Hutus meeting at a suspiciously odd hour in a suspiciously inconspicuous place."

"How did all this come to light?"

"In the course of an investigation that I have been conducting since shortly before dawn this morning, when several Hutus delivered Monsieur Curry to the hospital where you found him."

I didn't have any trouble picking up the implications of that. If Thomas's incident had been nothing more than disorderly conduct and aggravated battery, an official at Mboya's level wouldn't have gotten out of bed to look into it.

"It sounds like the Hutus took quite a risk to scrape Thomas up and get him to the hospital after the Watusi got through with him," I said. "I wonder why."

" 'The enemy of my enemy is my friend.' But the critical point, I think, is that they must have intervened *before* the Watusi got through with him. I think the attackers had something more permanent than a concussion in mind for Monsieur Curry."

"Hutus saved Thomas by physically attacking Watusi?" I asked. I was a long way from being an expert on Burundi, but I knew that Hutus were supposed to be too cowed to try anything like that.

"They were cornered," Mboya said. "Hutu secret meetings are illegal. They had little choice but to fight."

"They could've run while the Watusi were occupied with Thomas," I said.

"Sooner or later, people get tired of running."

The pronouncement came out flat and tired. I nodded a little to show I understood.

"You see what I am driving at?" Mboya asked me.

"I think so. Devereaux told Thomas that there are nine Hutus in Burundi for every Tutsi. You have to wonder when Hutus all over the country are going to get tired of running."

"I know perfectly well what will happen," Mboya said. "If a rebellion breaks out, the rebels will run out of Hutus before the soldiers run out of bullets."

"Yet you seem concerned."

"Soldiers can suppress a rebellion easily enough. But one cannot build a nation on piles of corpses. I want Burundi to be an African *nation*—not a quaint vestige of colonialism, with streets and buildings named after European saints and an anthem vaguely recalling the 'Marseillaise.' ''

"You're telling me you have a lot more at stake in this mess than clearing a foreigner's murder and sorting out a fight," I said. Being an experienced negotiator, I wondered if this was the right psychological moment to spring the information about Sandy's apparent disappearance. I decided to hold onto it for a bit.

"When was the last time you were in contact with Monsieur Curry?" Mboya asked.

"Last night."

"Before or after the reception at the French Embassy?"

"Long before, I assume. It was well before midnight. Why?"

"I was wondering whether he said anything that might shed light on why he was attacked."

"All he said was that he needed my help."

Mboya came forward and planted his right elbow on his desk.

"One obvious inference, at least if Major Ndala ordered the attack, is that he thought that Monsieur Curry knew something about the Hanson murder."

"No doubt." It took a conscious effort on my part not to shrug.

"And you of course see the significance of this," Mboya said. I didn't. "If Major Ndala thinks that Monsieur Curry knows something, then it is certain that he *could* know something, and it is possible that he *does* know it."

"Something that he learned at the embassy reception?"

"Exactly."

"I see."

"I wish to use you, Monsieur Furst."

"How?"

"I want you to secure Monsieur Curry's complete and unqualified cooperation with me. The investigation has reached the point where that cooperation is indispensable."

The right psychological moment had come.

"You've told me what's at stake in this from your standpoint. Let me tell you what's at stake from mine," I said.

Mboya held up his hand, palm out.

"No, Monsieur Furst, allow me to tell you." He punched a button on his telephone. The polite young man who'd picked me up at the hospital stepped through the door.

"Please fill Monsieur Furst in on the movements of Madame Sandrine Curry since early this morning," Mboya told him.

The young man extracted a thick, palm-size notebook from his inside coat pocket, flipped it open, and began to read in an understated, nothing-but-the-facts monotone:

"Between 4:15 and 4:30 this morning, presumably after a call from the hospital, Madame Curry left the Hotel Spaak and traveled by cab to Saint Vincent de Paul Hospital, where she saw her husband and ascertained that he was in a coma. She returned directly to the hotel, arriving back there at approximately 5:30. She appeared in the hotel lobby again just after 6:45. She was dressed casually, carrying a suitcase and a large handbag. She cashed several travelers' checks with the concierge, receiving ten thousand French francs and one thousand American dollars."

As if on cue, the man paused in his reading and swallowed, giving Mboya a chance to raise his eyebrows at me. The term "hard currency" went through my mind as the recitation resumed.

"Madame Curry checked the suitcase with the bellman, retaining the handbag. After leaving some written material with the reception desk, she proceeded to the hotel restaurant, where she ate breakfast."

"Croissant with butter and tea with lemon but no sugar, right?" I asked.

"Exact. At 7:20, Madame Curry left the hotel and engaged a taxicab. She paid the driver fifty French francs to be available to her exclusively for the remainder of the morning."

So that's how it's done, I thought.

"She took the cab to the agency of Monsieur Dray, where she arrived at 7:38. She was inside the agency for something over twenty-five minutes. At 8:05 Madame Curry was taken by her taxi to Saint Charles Foucald Catholic Church, which she reached at 8:21, in the midst of a service in progress at that time. She attended the remainder of the service, then after its conclusion spoke for not quite half an hour with the priest who had conducted it. The priest declined to say what was discussed in the course of the conference. She came back to her cab at 9:23."

I glanced at my watch. It was nearly four o'clock in the afternoon. At the rate things were going, I'd find out what Sandy had for lunch right around dinner time.

"The cab proceeded to take Madame Curry to the cabinet of Doctor François Duquesne. Arriving at approximately 9:45, she waited some twenty minutes to see him, consulted with him for an equivalent period, and left in the cab at 10:30. She was taken to the Vosges Pharmacy, which filled a prescription for Enovid given to her by Doctor Duquesne. She had completed this transaction by 11:02."

I kept my face absolutely expressionless. Sandrine Cadette Curry had picked up a supply of birth control pills. It'd take more than that to surprise me, my poker face said. After all, this is 1963. You could get them in New York without any trouble, and you could certainly get them anywhere grown-ups spoke French. Meanwhile, my mind was doing contortions trying to digest data that I couldn't even begin to believe.

"On her way back to the hotel, Madame Curry stopped at the LaTrobe Photographic Supply Outlet and purchased for cash a Koni Omega two-by-two format camera and a supply of black-and-white film for it. She arrived back at the hotel at 11:54."

He stopped. I waited. Finally it seemed to me that some prompting was in order.

"And?" I asked.

"Ah, Madame Curry went to the hotel restaurant and ordered lunch. The suitcase she had checked was still with the bellman. When she had not returned to the lobby from the restaurant by 12:50, it was determined that she had in fact exited the restaurant through its patio door around 12:20 and never returned."

It was determined, I thought. He couldn't bring himself to say, "She faked me out with the suitcase and I lost her." I didn't blame him.

"Reliable witnesses," the man continued, "later reported that sometime before 12:30 someone resembling Madame

104

Curry climbed into a Landrover being driven by a white male answering the description of Laurent Dray. Their present whereabouts is unknown."

What I thought about that was, in those innocent days, unprintable.

21

Thomas's reaction as I passed on this information and watched him study Sandy's note baffled me. I expected to see in his eyes incomprehension, fury, despair, passion, desperate disbelief—nineteenth-century stuff like that. Instead I saw intrigued surprise alloyed with mild puzzlement, like a prep school English master reacting to a second-former's unexpectedly penetrating comment on Hardy.

His expression wasn't the only thing baffling me. The dilemma I was wrestling with was as interesting intellectually as it was wrenching emotionally. On the one hand, as we lawyers say, what Mboya's legman had told me couldn't possibly be true. On the other hand, it couldn't possibly be false.

One failed marriage and fifteen-plus years of commercial law had cured me of wishful thinking. The facts seemed to speak for themselves. Thomas had hinted at a disagreement between him and Sandy the first time he'd called me from Burundi. Sandy's disappearance, the note she'd left, the story at the hotel about her fight with Thomas last night—all of that corroborated the report I'd just heard in Mboya's office. Those were facts—cold, hard, real-world facts. Looking at them from every imaginable angle, I could only come up with one way to read the message Sandy had had me deliver to Thomas.

Which was all fine, except that we were talking about Sandrine Cadette Curry. There are things that are out of character for someone, and then there are things that are just flat out impossible. For Sandy to storm off in a fit of passion, surrender to an emotional impulse after a bitter fight during a trying period—that would've been out of character, highly unlikely, hard to believe, but it could've happened. For Sandy methodically to betray Thomas while he was lying unconscious with a rainbow-colored face—forget it.

Which was all fine, except how else could I explain all those facts? Those nasty, stinking little facts?

So sitting beside Thomas's hospital bed around five-thirty in the evening, trying to decipher his almost surreal detachment, I waited for him to say something that would clear everything up for me. I was disappointed.

"Well, I'd better get in touch with whoever's in charge," Thomas said. He said this about the way you'd say *I think I'll try the veal for lunch next Tuesday.* "It'll probably take me an hour to talk my way out of here, and I don't have a lot of time to waste."

"You're less than fourteen hours from a severe concussion," I said. "And I can tell you from personal experience that no one's going to be talking their way past the nun who runs this place. Her favorite word is *impossible.* You'd better plan on being here at least overnight. Anything you want done before tomorrow I'll do."

Thomas's reactions seemed about two beats slower than usual. He considered my comment for a very long moment before he turned his bandaged head deliberately toward me with a you-asked-for-it expression on his face.

"Fair enough, Theodore." He paused uncharacteristically to take a breath. "First, please go to the Hotel Spaak and retrieve the suitcase Sandy checked. Inside I expect you'll find a Pentax single-lens reflex camera. I'd like you to bring it here."

"I'll try," I shrugged.

"Second, while you're out and about, I'd appreciate it if

107

you'd contact Mboya. Tell him that I'd like to see Devereaux tomorrow and find out if he's willing to arrange it."

"Okay," I said. "Sure."

I coughed. The cough was dry and nervous.

"Was there something else?" Thomas asked.

Yes, there was something else. When a lawyer's in doubt he hedges his bets. I was in doubt.

"I checked with the airport in Stanleyville," I said.

"Commendable initiative. Why is Stanleyville important?"

"It's the biggest city anywhere near the Congo's border with Burundi. If you want a plane to Europe and you can't fly out of Bujumbura, Stanleyville's where you'd go."

"Okay," Thomas shrugged. "What'd you find out?"

"There won't be any foreign flights from Stanleyville until noon tomorrow at the earliest. I've been looking into charters from Bujumbura. If I leave by midnight tonight I can be in Stanleyville before anyone could catch a flight from there to anywhere outside the Congo."

I said this as delicately as I could. Making all possible allowances for the power of psychological denial, Thomas's serene passivity still struck me as pathetically feckless. What was going on wasn't clear, but what might be going on was obvious. To take some elementary precautions only made sense, and I thought I should try to make him see that while there was still time to do something constructive.

It didn't work.

"Theodore," Thomas said, "my marriage isn't in danger. My wife is." His voice had found an edge, and his eyes suddenly glinted with the first suggestion of intensity I'd seen there since my arrival in Burundi.

"If that's so," I coaxed, "then—"

"It is so. Sandy's telling me the place I can help her is here. So that's what I'm going to do. And I need you here to help me."

We looked at each other for five very long and very silent seconds.

"Sure, buddy," I said then. I squeezed his hand and left as quickly as I could. My shoulders drooped a little on the way out.

                            *   *   *

Sandy, at just about that moment, sat in the Landrover.
Motionless and shielded by tall grass and brush, the vehicle
sat on a downslope well off the road in the Congolese high-
lands, roughly four kilometers from the Burundi border. Late
afternoon sunlight glared whitely from the hood.

When Sandy braved the glare long enough to glance
through the windshield, she could glimpse Dray lying beside
the road on the crest of the slope some fifty meters ahead of the
Landrover. Dray gazed through binoculars at the countryside
behind them. He had been looking for twenty minutes, pan-
ning the glasses patiently along the horizon in small arcs and
sedulously examining each segment before he moved on to the
next one.

Lowering the binoculars, Dray massaged his eyes with the
thumb and middle finger of his right hand. He recased the
glasses, rolled a few meters down the slope, then came to his
feet and trotted in a crouching lope back toward the Landrover.

He is careful, Sandy thought. Even more noticeable here
than when he was guiding Thomas and me in Burundi. Interesting to spend time with a careful man.

"No activity," he reported as he slid back behind the
Landrover's wheel. "We should be all right now until at least
nightfall. If they were going to try anything in this sector
during daylight they would have done it before the guard
changed at the border post."

The Landrover coughed to life. Dray guided it along the
slope at almost a forty-degree angle, their course well below
and parallel to the road above them.

"Will we be able to reach Kasongo tonight?" Sandy
asked.

Dray shook his head.

"Both sides shoot too quickly at night when things are the
way they are in the Congo now," he explained. "We will have
to find a place to camp before nightfall and plan on Kasongo
for sometime tomorrow."

"*Bien,*" Sandy shrugged.

They had churned another ten kilometers into the Congo
when Dray nosed the Landrover delicately up the slope.

"Why are we going back to the road?" Sandy asked.

                              109

"Listen," Dray told her.

Straining, Sandy could just make out the distant hum of a helicopter to the southwest.

"One cannot hide from copters," Dray explained. "And if one cannot hide, it is very bad to be seen trying to do so."

Sandy nodded.

The Landrover chugged onto the road. It had proceeded less than a hundred meters when the copter came into sight, not much more than a black speck at first, then rapidly growing as it swung toward them.

Dray took his hat off and swept it slowly over his head from left to right—a casual greeting that not even the jumpiest troops could misinterpret as a call for help. The helicopter waggled its landing skids at Dray and continued to move toward them.

Dray pulled the Landrover to a stop. Standing up on the seat, Dray deliberately waved the hat in three exaggerated figure eights to his left, paused, then did another left figure eight, a right figure eight, and a final left figure eight: Morse code for OK. The copter's skids waggled again and the helicopter banked off to the south, pulling away from them.

Sandy glanced at her watch as the Landrover lurched once more into motion. It was now after six o'clock. They had been traveling for over five hours. Between delicate, probing approaches to the border, occasional stops to reconnoiter, and the slow speed required by unforgiving terrain, she doubted that they'd covered seventy kilometers.

They stopped just before 8:00 P.M. in a modest copse of yew trees. From the back of the Landrover, Dray extracted a compact Sweda paraffin stove, no more than eight inches high and only slightly larger than his hand.

"Can we risk a fire?" Sandy asked.

"Not a fire, certainly, but enough of a flame for this little item."

Setting up the miniature stove on the Landrover's hood, he deftly pulled the paraffin block out of its base and lit the wick with his lighter.

"There," he said, slipping the block back into position and half filling the aluminum cup above it with water from his canteen. "Not exactly Escoffier, but in a few minutes we can at least enjoy a hot meal."

"Give me a task, if you please," Sandy asked.

"See if you can find a can of pork and beans and the opener over there on the other side of the boot," Dray said, nodding toward the Landrover's storage compartment.

While Sandy searched, Dray took out a tin camp fry pan and balanced it on the stove's cup. Noting that Sandy had found the items he'd asked for, he told her to open the can and pour the contents into the fry pan. She did so. By the time she'd finished Dray had rummaged in his knapsack and had come up with a tiny onion and a dwarf potato.

"Onion, meat, potato, beans," he told Sandy, grinning, as he handed her the vegetables and nodded at a fish fillet knife on the dashboard. "A balanced diet. Slice thin."

Sandy got to work, and Dray began to stir the now-sizzling mixture in the fry pan with the handle of a fork, swirling pork fragments through the beans and sauce. They were close enough to smell the sweat on each other's bodies and to hear each other's steady breathing.

A pungent, savory smell rose from the cooking food. A silken breeze from the west caressed their cheeks. In the gathering dusk, the vivid green leaves and bushes faded gradually to textured black, and the sere countryside seemed to radiate a luminous, orange-brown glow.

"Central Africa surprises me all over again every time I see it," Sandy mused as she scraped onion and potato bits into the pan. "The light itself seems to have a different quality at dusk than the light in Europe or America."

Dray nodded.

"A diplomat I know told me once that his two worst days in the service were the day he learned he'd been assigned to sub-Saharan Africa and the day he learned he'd be rotated home," Dray said.

"I know exactly how he felt."

They worked together without speaking again for several minutes. Only the spatter and pop of the cooking food interrupted the quiet. Then Dray fetched a tin plate from the mess kit and ladled half the bubbling meal from the fry pan onto it.

Handing the plate and a fork to Sandy, he kept the pan and a spoon for himself.

"The sleeping quarters in the Landrover are cramped, even with the seats folded down," Dray said with affected casualness after the first couple of mouthfuls.

"I should imagine," Sandy said. She looked searchingly at him.

"It is of no consequence at the moment, because one or the other of us will have to be keeping watch all night anyway. I can go first and wake you after midnight."

"*Je crois que non,*" Sandy said. "You would let me sleep while you struggled heroically through until morning. I will take the first watch. You can be certain I will wake you."

"You accuse me of gallantry, madame," Dray said, glancing up at her with a dry smile. "I ought to be gravely insulted."

" '*Horum omnium fortissimi sunt Belgae,* ' " Sandy answered, returning the teasing semismirk.

"One cannot take Caesar seriously," Dray said, shrugging at the allusion. "He was his own press agent."

It was after nine-thirty that night before I made it back to Thomas's bedside. I'd returned to the hospital by a bit after seven, but I'd run into a wall of *impossibles* when I tried to get in to see Thomas. I probably would've failed again when I came back more than two hours later, but by that time Thomas was making enough of a nuisance of himself that they let me in just to see if I could shut him up for a few minutes.

His eyes brightened the moment he saw the camera in my right hand.

"Well done, Theodore," he said, reaching out for it. Genuine spirit colored his voice.

I smiled gamely, doing my best to play along. I thought the world of Sandy, but an opinion's an opinion and facts are facts. During the hours I'd spent tracking around Bujumbura, the facts had gotten heavier in my mind, and the hopes more ephemeral.

He took the camera from me and opened the back, where I could see there wasn't any film. Setting the shutter speed at a full second, he cocked the shutter and pressed the release. The shutter's black curtain popped open, held for a second, then snapped closed. Thomas nodded judiciously at the camera's unremarkable mechanical functioning.

Turning the camera over, Thomas removed the lens. After examining that from both ends, Thomas repeated the shutter business while looking at the camera from the front. As nearly as I could tell, the shutter worked exactly the way it had the first time.

"Well, well," he said to himself. "Isn't that interesting?"

"It certainly is," I said. "What are you talking about?"

"The camera's working perfectly," he said, looking up at me. "The body's a little banged up from our adventure on the hilltop, and I suppose the telephoto lens won't ever be used again, but the standard lens is fine, and the camera itself is as good as the day we bought it."

"Fascinating," I muttered. I was starting to lose patience. "So what?"

"So," Thomas explained, "you know how Sandy is about money. Why would she drop over a hundred dollars on a new camera when the one she already had was still working?"

Maybe because it's your money, I thought bitterly, reflecting on my own less than pleasant experience at the end of my first marriage.

"You tell me," I said, instead of giving voice to this unconstructive speculation.

"I don't know," Thomas said. "But you can bet your Metropolitan Opera tickets there's a good reason. I'm beginning to look forward to this. Speaking of which, did you reach Mboya?"

"I reached his aide," I admitted. "He's supposed to check and leave a message for me at the hotel."

"Check tonight?" Thomas demanded.

I bobbed my head.

"The midnight oil is burning at the *Palais de Justice*," I said.

Thomas nodded decisively.

"He'll come through," he said. "Can you plan on picking me up first thing in the morning?"

I stood up, turned my back on Thomas, and paced a bit as I wiped the back of my neck with my right hand in frustration.

"This isn't like you, Thomas," I said.

"What isn't like me?"

"You're ignoring facts."

"On the contrary," Thomas said cheerfully, "I'm looking at all the facts instead of limiting myself to the more obvious ones."

I turned around to face him.

"The only nonobvious fact I've heard about so far is that Sandy bought a new camera even though the one she left behind was still okay," I said. "And you just told me you don't have any idea how that fits into anything else. Isn't it stretching things a bit to say that everything else we know means exactly the opposite of what it seems to mean?"

"Tell me something, Theodore," Thomas said. "How did you manage to get all the way through Yale Law School without learning to look at both sides of documents you were reviewing?" He held Sandy's note out to me as he completed the question.

I took the tendered page and examined its reverse side. I had to fiddle with my bifocals a little before I saw what he was talking about. Outlined faintly in pencil on the quadrille-lined lab-report paper was a diagram of some kind. After a bit of examination, I satisfied myself that it was a floor plan.

"That's a schematic of the Muramvya hostelry where the murder took place," Thomas said.

"You're suggesting that this is the real message Sandy left for you," I said. "Or at least that the real message can only be understood in light of this."

"What do you think?" Thomas asked.

"You want the truth? Pascal said the heart has its reasons, and you're proving it. I think you're rationalizing. You're wishing away inconvenient facts so you can go with your gut."

"Gut's just another word for faith, you know," Thomas said, his voice quiet and thoughtful. "If Pascal were as smart as he thought he was, he would've said the *cran* has its reasons."

"There's a big difference between guts and brains," I murmured.

"Only a single letter in French," Thomas said. He grinned.

His optimism was contagious. I hesitated mentally for a moment, and that was enough for a slight flicker of the hope Thomas was husbanding to ignite in me. I began to imagine that, as we were having that very conversation, Sandy might not be spending the night with a man intent on taking her away from her spouse.

"That crack sounds like something Sandy might've said," I commented a bit wistfully.

"It is," Thomas assured me in the same quietly confident tone.

22

Sandy tasted the acrid smoke before she saw it, two hours after dawn and still forty kilometers from Kasongo. The Landrover had just entered a curve when the smoke's bitter savor first scorched her throat.

As they finished rounding the curve, Sandy glimpsed dark gray streamlets trailing from the ground to the sky two hundred meters or so off the road, calling attention to the charred remains of what had been a stockade-type fence and a handful of wooden buildings. No bodies were visible, but the stench of human death hung unmistakably over the scene. A sign reading L'HÔPITAL DE LA PETITE FLEUR, warped and darkened but not destroyed, still stood mockingly near what had presumably been the gate through the fence.

Sandy tried to blink the stinging smoke out of her tearing eyes.

"Last night?" she asked.

"Must have been," Dray answered. "We can at least be thankful that the attackers are busily getting as far away from here as they can. The peacekeeping force will have started its search from the point of the attack."

Sandy nodded.

How many had died there last night? she wondered. How many had been raped? How many victims among people who had never gotten a *sou* for themselves out of whatever wealth Belgium had extracted from the Congo; people whose only contribution to colonial exploitation had been to give medicine and care to Congolese; defenseless people who had been murdered and violated for no other reason than that they had white skin and spoke French?

"How much longer to Kasongo?" she asked.

"Three more hours," Dray said. "If we are lucky."

"Yes," Sandy murmured. "That contingency is understood."

23

"Understand one thing from the start," I said to Devereaux. "I don't care about you or your problems. I don't care whether you hang for a crime you didn't commit or get off scot-free on a crime you did commit. *Je ne m'en fiche pas.*"

"Then why are you here?" Devereaux asked, in a tone suggesting he was as indifferent to me as I professed to be to him.

"Because I do care about my client, Thomas Andrew Curry," I said. "I've concluded that the Burundi climate is unhealthy for him. I want to get him out."

"*Je ne m'en fiche pas,*" Devereaux said, showing tobacco-stained teeth in a brief, malicious smile.

"Well, you'd better start giving a damn about it," I said.

"Tell me why."

I took my right thumb out of my vest pocket as I rocked minimally back toward the cell window. I didn't really enjoy playing the heavy in a situation like this. What little knowledge I had about Devereaux left me with a sneaking sympathy for his plight and even a grudging admiration for the man himself. Besides, in the moderately civilized, more or less upper-class institutions where I'd been educated, I'd been taught that you don't kick someone when he's down. Thomas and I had talked this over for an hour, though, and we'd agreed that there wasn't any other way to play it. We just weren't holding enough aces to keep on being the only nice guys at the table.

Credit for having me instead of Thomas come to see Devereaux goes to Mboya. Thomas at the moment was sitting in the café at the Hotel Spaak, reading a copy of the *International Herald Tribune* and drinking a cup of coffee. A uniformed officer of the Bujumbura Judicial Police stood at parade rest in the café doorway, his eyes riveted on Thomas. Another officer stood at the doorway from the café to the patio. They were there to make sure that Thomas didn't leave the hotel or do anything inside it without a well-armed audience. It was a combination of protective custody and house arrest. Mboya had made it clear that this arrangement was not negotiable.

"Curry learned something about you at the French Embassy the night he was attacked," I said, beginning my answer to Devereaux's last question.

"What did he learn?"

"I don't know."

"Your client does not trust you enough to share this critical information with you?" Devereaux demanded with mocking sarcasm. "How remarkable."

"I don't know because I told Curry not to tell me," I said. "What he learned made Major Ndala want to kill him. If I knew it, Major Ndala might want to kill me, too."

"A plausible response. I understand that an *avocat* is someone with more brains than *cran*."

I shrugged.

"I believe Mboya would like to know what Curry learned," I said. "I suspect he's anxious enough to find it out that he'll let Curry leave if Curry will just tell him."

"Then your course is clear," Devereaux said. He said it nonchalantly, but he was a half second slow. His expression during that momentary hesitation told me that he didn't relish

119

the idea of Thomas going to Mboya with the unknown information I'd alluded to.

"Clear to me," I said, "but not to Curry. He's willing to stay quiet about whatever he's learned if you'll tell him what was really going on between you and Ndala. He figures that's what has to be behind this whole sorry mess. He's convinced himself that you're innocent, and he feels he owes it to his wife to try to keep you from being railroaded."

"A nice sentiment," Devereaux rejoined. "Particularly since Madame Curry has as I understand been, ah, called away unexpectedly and ah, on short notice. And without Monsieur Curry."

"Exactly the point, I suspect," I said. "I think he's trying to impress her."

"Probably a misguided effort."

"Maybe, maybe not. If he can show Sandy that there actually is more to your tawdry situation than meets the eye, that might be enough to coax her back here so she can pitch in. That's the kind of attitude you were banking on from the beginning, and he's betting she still has it."

"You mean that to save my own neck I have to preserve this rich American's marriage?" Devereaux demanded. "I'm not sure it's worth it."

"It's your decision. Thomas's instructions are to give you until noon to come across with the real story. If you do, he'll keep his mouth shut and do his best to get Sandy back here to help you. If you don't, I call Mboya to see if I can make a deal with him."

Striding across the cell, I clanged on the door to summon the guard.

"Do you really expect me to agree to this?" Devereaux asked. He was looking directly at the wall across the cell from him instead of at me.

"How can you refuse? I should have won you over by charm alone."

The guard showed up before Devereaux could answer. It's probably a good thing.

I felt like I'd won when I stepped out of the cell, but I was far from sure. All the way back to the hotel I wondered whether I'd actually sold the bluff. Thomas was waiting for me in the lobby, and as soon as I saw his face I knew the answer.

"Mboya called," he told me. "Devereaux asked to see him five minutes after you left."

24

The howitzer's occasional blasts echoed at Checkpoint Hercules like distant, muted thunder. Sandy figured that the field piece must by now be three kilometers beyond the hastily erected sandbag and barbed-wire barrier where six Ghurkas under a UN flag had detained her and Dray for nearly two hours now. Shifting her hindquarters in the dirt where she sat and pressing her shoulders against the Landrover's right rear tire, she shielded her eyes from the midmorning sun and concentrated on Guy Montherlant's *Conceptual Approach to Physical Geography*—one of only three books she had brought along with her. As perspiration ran down her neck from behind her ears, she began to think that Montherlant had given insufficient attention to the importance of climate.

Dray bounded toward her from an olive drab tent that served as the Ghurkas' command post. Sandy sensed a spring in Dray's rapid strides as she heard him approach. She glanced up at him optimistically.

"They have finally decided to let us proceed," he said, confirming her hopes. "In fact, now that the military convoy is well past this point, the sooner we are on our way the happier they will be."

"At last," Sandy said, smiling luminously at Dray as she came to her feet. "How far are we from Kasongo?"

Before answering, Dray paused for a moment to enjoy her. He regarded himself as a connoisseur of feminine pleasure. With deepening satisfaction, he thought that he saw Sandy glowing not merely with happiness but also with excitement. He very much looked forward to the rest of the day.

"Twelve kilometers, with a decent road the rest of the way," he told her, his voice resonant with anticipation. "If that cannon keeps firing in the opposite direction, we should reach Kasongo in fifteen minutes."

Thirteen minutes later they reached the sprawling town of some forty thousand people, swollen by the logistical backup for a peacekeeping force that was keeping peace at the moment by firing a howitzer and machine guns at Katangese rebels several kilometers to the north. The mostly single-story buildings on the small city's outskirts were grouped in irregular conglomerations, as if they'd been thrown up in haphazard spasms of construction activity. Not until they were a kilometer inside the perimeter did they see some kind of order begin to emerge along narrow, winding, stone-paved streets.

Dray skirted a plaza in the center of the city, driving past what gave every promise of being the only hotel in town with any pretension to elegance. Patiently negotiating the tedious traffic on the other side of the plaza, he guided the Landrover through street markets and past alleys that stank of raw sewage until they reached a broader road separated from a sluggish green river by a row of thirteen curved-roof warehouses.

The third warehouse from the far end of the street had a faded mural of a tropical bird in a jungle setting painted over its wide door. Just short of the drive leading to that door, Dray pulled the Landrover to a stop and waited. He glanced apologetically at Sandy, apparently expecting a question or a protest from her. Instead of interrogating him, though, Sandy swiveled in her seat, glancing around in an effort to take in the scene without missing anything.

After nearly three minutes, two shirtless black men pushed the warehouse door laboriously open. Dray turned right onto the short driveway and swung the Landrover through the opening, driving it well into the building's dark recesses. Dry heat radiated from wooden walls.

A quarter of the way down the length of the building, Dray eased the vehicle over toward the nearer wall, pulling it into a space about two meters from a muddy Ford pickup truck with a khaki canvas draped on arched ribs over its bed.

"Only four hours late," a voice that Sandy identified as American said in English from the back of the Ford. "For you, that's practically on time."

"My ambition is to grow old in the guide business," Dray responded as he jumped to the floor. "There is a war on, or hadn't you heard?"

Sandy looked around in time to see a stocky, well-muscled man just under two meters in height leap heavily from the back of the pickup. He looked like he was in his late twenties or early thirties. His face was deeply tanned, his hair jet black and worn medium length.

"Glad you made it, you ugly old frog," he said as he gripped Dray's hand tightly and slapped his shoulder. He kept his jaw tightly clenched as he talked, and his mouth formed a dark, toothless slit.

"I am glad I made it also, you loudmouthed Yank," Dray said affectionately. He moved his head minutely in Sandy's direction. "And before you say anything else, remember that you are in a civilized country, not at some waterfront dive in San Francisco."

"Okay," the man said, smiling. "So? That mean I'm not supposed to ask about your, ah—guest, would it be?"

Dray stepped back and gestured broadly toward Sandy with his left arm.

"Allow me to introduce Madame Sandrine Cadette Curry," he said. "And 'guest' will do nicely."

"That says it all, then. Glad to know you," the man said to Sandy.

"The pleasure is mine," Sandy said. "And you would of course be Monsieur Kerry Travis, no?"

"Naturally," the man said. "Who else would I be?"

25

"Would you like me to take a walk?" Sandy asked, smiling at the awkward silence that suddenly intervened between the two men as soon as the introductions were finished.

"On the contrary," Dray said lightly, "I have no intention of letting you out of my sight."

"You are not afraid that I will learn something dangerous if I stay?"

"Nothing you might learn by staying will be as dangerous as what you already know, which is that there is something here to be learned."

"All right already," the American said. "Let's get it done."

He took a wad of currency of different shapes, sizes, and colors from inside his shirt and handed it to Dray. Dropping to one knee, Dray spread the money on the floor. The hoard included an array of denominations in old and new French francs, dollars, Belgian francs, deutsche marks, Swiss francs, pounds, and even two richly glowing gold Krugerrands.

"Very nice," Dray said as he fetched a worn leather document envelope from the Landrover and began to slip the carefully sorted money into it. "But we are a bit short, are we not?"

"Can't be helped." Shrug. "We're moving heavy inventory in a falling market. I have to give you the rest in barter."

"What barter?" Dray demanded.

Following a nod from his companion, Dray sprang up and looked into the sheltered back of the pickup. Looking bored, Sandy heard what sounded like heavy fabric scraping over wood, followed by the sharply protesting crack of a crate-lid being pried partially open. A cold, wet finger of fear plunged into her stomach. Shielded from what Dray was seeing by the pickup's canvas cover, she ostentatiously made no effort to get a better view.

"How much altogether?" Dray asked.

"Half-a-skid worth."

"Still light, no?"

"I forgot to mention I'm throwing in the truck."

Dray's eyes darted upward barely in time for him to snatch the key chain that the other man tossed at him.

"What am I going to do with a truck?" Dray asked, almost laughing with incredulity.

"How should I know? Find a Zulu somewhere with a driver's license and no fear. He'll think of something."

"In other words, you are liquidating your capital at my expense."

"You got that exactly right. Consider it liquidated. As of right now. What you've got you've got, and what I've got I keep. Sixteen hundred hours today I'm off on the first leg of a trip that isn't going to stop 'til I'm back in one of those waterfront dives in 'Frisco you talked about. I'm not taking anything I can't carry in one hand."

"If this discussion is going to go on much longer, Monsieur Travis," Sandy interjected, "perhaps we could continue it at the hotel over a drink and something to eat."

"I think I'll skip the hotel, if it's all the same with you. Three's a crowd, as we say in the States."

"No more of a crowd at a restaurant than here, and at a restaurant at least one-third of this particular crowd will be less likely to die of famine."

"Madame Curry is entirely correct," Dray said. "If I have to get rolled, I'd rather not do it on an empty stomach."

"You're not getting rolled, froggie—"

"Good. Then you will have no objection to going over the figures with me. In detail. It promises to be thirsty work."

"Have it your way," the American sighed, grinning and shaking his head. "But you can pay for the cab."

"*Bien*. You can pay for the drinks and the meal."

Sandy began to pull an olive drab duffel bag from the Landrover as the other two started for the door.

"You can leave all that," Dray said, looking back over his shoulder. "It will be entirely safe here, and we can send porters back for it from the hotel."

" 'You can leave all that,' " Sandy mimicked, sighing in mock exasperation. "Easy enough for a man to say." She extracted the duffel bag and looped the strap over her right shoulder.

"Suit yourself," Dray said, his voice warm and affectionate.

"I have a feeling that that's exactly what she intends to do, my little Belgian buddy," the other man whispered.

The trip from the warehouse to the King Leopold Hotel took not quite twice as long as that morning's journey from Checkpoint Hercules into Kasongo. When they finally spilled out of their taxi onto the crowded plaza in front of the hotel, its veranda seemed incongruous, like something from a Catskills resort that had inexplicably turned up on Central Park West.

"I have a service to ask of you, Monsieur Travis," Sandy said as Dray paid the cab driver.

"You're pretty used to getting what you want, aren't you?" he asked. He directed this question to the back of her head, because Sandy had stooped to unzip the duffel bag.

"*Je crois que oui*," Sandy answered. She pulled a tripod and the Koni Omega from the bag. "It is a question of knowing when to ask, I think."

"What are you doing now, playing tourist?" Dray asked as he turned around to see Sandy setting the tripod up on the plank sidewalk in front of the hotel.

"In a manner of speaking," Sandy said. Mounting the camera on the tripod, she flipped the top open to expose the Koni's ground glass, in which she could now see a gray image of a huge bay window with KING LEOPOLD HOTEL etched on it in arching, gilt letters. "I would like monsieur Travis to take a picture that I have been planning since we drove past this hotel this morning."

"Cameras aren't one of my occupational specialties," the American demurred. "I'll probably just mess it up."

"I will set everything," Sandy said, fiddling with lens openings and shutter speeds as she did so. "All you have to do is stand behind the camera and push a button."

"I don't *have* to do anything."

"Of course not," Sandy said. "I mean, of course, all that I am asking you to do." She turned toward Dray. "Indulge me," she said to him. "It will take you less time to do it than to talk me out of it, and if we do it I promise not to pout for the rest of the afternoon."

"Sometime," Dray sighed as Sandy cajoled him onto the veranda, "I must make it a point to see you pout. But today is not the day."

His smile forced and embarrassed, gamely confronting the smirk of his American business partner, Dray took up the position Sandy pointed out to him, directly in front of the window, his head just blocking the o's and the P in LEOPOLD. Sandy stood beside him. She wrapped her left arm around his waist. Almost shyly at first, Dray stretched his right arm behind Sandy's back, cupping her right shoulder in his hand. The moment he felt her respond to the affectionate gesture, he softened. His features relaxed into the self-confidence natural to them.

"The button on the front, near the upper right-hand corner, Monsieur Travis," Sandy called.

The shutter snapped.

"Thank you," Sandy said.

"No problem."

"Can we go into the hotel now?" Dray asked.

"Of course." Sandy kissed him on the cheek. "You have been very sweet."

Dray registered and hired three porters to bring the rest of

128

their baggage from the warehouse while Sandy secured a table in the small, dimly lit café. Dray joined them at the table in time to learn from the waiter that the only thing on the menu that day was pork royale and Tusker beer.

"For three," Dray shrugged. "Now," he said as the waiter retreated. "About the numbers."

Wordlessly, the American dug a greasy, much-folded sheaf of papers out of his pants and handed them across the table. Dray was less than ten minutes into his scrutiny of the scrawled figures when the waiter approached with three covered plates. It seemed to Sandy to be much too soon for pork royale.

It was. At least that day, pork royale at the King Leopold Hotel was two slabs of Spam with cream of chicken soup ladled over them.

"The prospect of San Francisco must be more and more enticing, Monsieur Travis," Sandy said.

"Fortunes of war," he answered. "There've been lots of times in 'Frisco when I'd have sold my soul for a slice of Spam."

Sandy, who believed in finishing disagreeable tasks as quickly as possible, polished off her Spam and beer long before Dray had completed his run-through of the pages tendered to him.

"If you will be kind enough to give me the room key," Sandy said, "I will excuse myself and freshen up while you complete your discussion."

"I will try not to be too long," Dray said. He smiled as he turned the key over to her.

"I intend to hold you to that." Rising, she kissed him on the forehead and headed for the lobby.

Dray had gotten a front room for them, one flight up from the ground floor. Sandy worried the door open, stepped inside, and confirmed that a bellhop had brought up her duffel bag and deposited it on the bed. Closing the door, she went immediately to the bathroom.

A copper washbowl and pitcher stood on a varnished wood cabinet underneath the mirror. Sandy looked at herself in the glass. She poured some water into the bowl. She splashed water on her face, tentatively at first, then used her cupped hands to soak her face and neck liberally.

Again she looked at herself in the mirror. She took a deep breath. Interesting to see fear and betrayal at the same time in one's own eyes, she thought. After glancing at her watch, she took out the hard plastic pill case she'd picked up about twenty-four hours before at the Bujumbura pharmacy.

She extracted an Enovid from the case and swallowed it.

26

"My problems began when Major Ndala decided that I'd shorted him on a financial transaction."

Devereaux's lifeless voice came to Thomas and me over a desktop intercom, one office away from Mboya's. The flat tones contrasted sharply with the verve he'd displayed when I'd talked to him in his cell a couple of hours earlier. Something vital seemed to have gone out of him after he'd decided to throw in the towel and spill his guts to Mboya.

"What transaction was that?" Mboya asked Devereaux.

"It is not material."

"Tell me about it anyway."

Devereaux's sigh was almost audible in the white-noise silence that came over the intercom for a long moment. There wasn't any fight left in him.

"I was supposed to collect some money for Ndala from a guy called Tsivimbi."

"Who is Tsivimbi?"

"He claims to be a colonel."

"Burundi armed forces?" Mboya asked.

"Katanga *gendarmerie.*"

"And what was the money for?"

"Your guess is as good as mine."

"My guess," Mboya said speculatively, his voice suggesting no irritation at Devereaux's evasion, "would be that it was paid in consideration for Major Ndala overlooking the presence of Tsivimbi's men on Burundi soil from time to time."

"Such a thing is certainly possible," Devereaux agreed.

"What went wrong?"

"Tsivimbi gave me less than he was supposed to. I pointed this out to him, and he said that was all he had. When I turned the money over to Ndala, I told him what had happened."

"But Ndala refused to accept your explanation?"

"He accused me of skimming off part of Tsivimbi's payment for myself. Our discussion of this issue quickly reached an impasse. Ndala had me court-martialed *in absentia* on imaginary charges and sentenced to death."

"The *in absentia* aspect puzzles me a bit," Mboya said. "This discussion you said you had with Ndala about Tsivimbi's money—was that face-to-face or through intermediaries?"

"Face-to-face. Not by my choice. Believe it, I would cheerfully have handled the whole thing through the mail. Ndala's men insisted on a personal audience. Inasmuch as they had me by the throat at the time, I was in no position to demur."

"Very well, then. Ndala has you physically in his clutches. He has accused you of keeping part of Tsivimbi's money for yourself, and he has rejected your version of events. Why didn't he just hang on to you?"

"Hang on to me is exactly what he did do," Devereaux said. "He held me in uncomfortably close confinement."

"If he had you in custody, why did he try you *in absentia?*"

"Precisely because trying me in person would have disclosed the fact that he had me in custody. Given what Major Ndala had in mind for me, revealing that he had me in custody at the time of the court-martial would have required him to explain how I happened to be free a bit later. Major Ndala, I gather, anticipated that such an explanation would be tedious.

By trying me *in absentia,* as if I had been at large all the time, he would be able to dispense with it."

During the brief pause that followed, I glanced at Thomas, who was supplementing his own limited understanding of the French exchange by studying the detailed notes I was taking. I'd been surprised to learn that Mboya had notified Thomas about his impending interview with Devereaux and invited both of us to attend. For him to check what Devereaux said against what Thomas knew made sense. But he didn't need to have us on the scene listening to the interrogation to do that. I couldn't help thinking that he had an ulterior motive. The more I thought about it the less I liked it.

" 'What Major Ndala had in mind for me,' " Mboya repeated after a thoughtful interlude. "What did he have in mind for you?"

"Ndala held me for about three weeks. Then one night his men came for me, and I thought, this is it. Instead of taking me to the basement of Sainte Jeanne to be shot, though, they brought me to Ndala."

"What happened then?"

"Ndala said, 'In Muramvya there is an American named Alex Hanson. I want this man killed. I want you to kill him. Will you do this?' "

"Exact words?"

"I am not likely to forget them."

"What did you answer?" Mboya asked in an even, undramatic voice.

"What do you think?"

"I think nothing. I want you to tell me. What did you answer when Major Ndala asked you if you would kill Alex Hanson?"

"I said of course I would," Devereaux spat. For the first time in the interview his voice showed a trace of animation. "What else could I say?"

"And so you proceeded to Muramvya and shot Alex Hanson under the duress represented by Major Ndala's threat. Is that the way it was?"

"No."

On my pad I emphatically underlined the note I made of

that answer. Devereaux hadn't fallen into Mboya's trap. Duress isn't a defense to a capital crime.

"Tell me how it happened then," Mboya said to Devereaux.

"Ndala gave me a ticket on the bus to Muramvya and showed me a picture of Hanson. He said that once I got to the scene one of his men would show me where Hanson was and provide me with a gun."

"Showed you a picture? You mean you did not know Hanson?"

"I had never seen him or heard of him."

"Continue."

"I got on the bus," Devereaux resumed. "The attack and the aftermath you know about. It came as a surprise to me, but by then I was used to unpleasant surprises. When the soldiers finally got us to Muramvya, I found myself assigned to share Hanson's room, and Hanson himself was quite conveniently there, waiting for me."

"Are you certain it was Hanson in the room?"

"I am certain it was the man whose picture Ndala had shown me and whom Ndala's man identified as the person I was supposed to kill."

"Did the picture Ndala showed you resemble this one?" Mboya asked, as I imagined a photograph being slipped across the desk.

"They appear to be identical."

"Very well," Mboya said after a brief, contemplative grunt. "Go on."

"One of the subofficers slipped me an American .45 pistol. He told me that there'd be some kind of diversion just before dawn the following morning. I surmised that I was to take care of Hanson then."

"But you acted before that time?" Mboya prompted.

"No. I did not act at all until it was too late. I wasted too much time trying to figure which way to play it."

"What options did you consider?"

"I thought it out this way: On the one hand, if I killed Hanson my account with Ndala was square, and I was supposed to get six hundred French francs to boot."

"Ndala had promised you this?"

134

"Yes."

"On the other hand, then?"

"On the other hand, I knew I was being set up."

"I suppose one thing you might have done was tell Hanson what was going on and see if you could work together to get yourselves out of the jam you were both in," Mboya said.

"I rejected that course as too risky. If Hanson decided I was crazy and talked things over with Ndala, I was in the soup. If he made a break for it, that was bad too. If he reacted by killing me before I could kill him, that was the worst of all."

"So what did you decide to do?"

"I determined to get up two hours before dawn and sneak off. My plan was to make my way to the Congo and lie low there until things in Burundi were clearer."

"How did you plan to get past the guards?" Mboya asked.

"Exactly the way I did get past them—or would have, if Madame Curry had not been lying in the middle of the porch."

"Ah. You had worked things out ahead of time."

"Of course. I had the pillow stuffed in my shirt and trousers before I ever went to sleep. I talked with Hanson a bit to see if I could pry any information out of him. I couldn't. I got plenty of dried dates from him but no answers. I'd had a long day, and I felt drowsy even before dark. I went to bed, and the next thing I remember is the sound of the gunshot waking me up. The rest happened the way I described it to Madame Curry, which I presume she passed on to you."

"I would like you to describe it to me," Mboya said in the same patient, implacable voice he'd been using throughout the interview.

Devereaux proceeded to run through the same account he'd given to Thomas and Sandy when they came to his cell.

"Repeat the part about the diversion and your escape," Mboya said when he'd finished.

"It was as I said. I already had my shirt and trousers ready, stuffed with the pillow. As soon as I'd collected my wits after the shot, I ripped the mosquito netting out of the way, threw the pillow out, and climbed up to the roof while the guard outside was riddling the pillow."

"You ripped the mosquito netting away?"

"That is what I said."

135

"You see the difficulty," Mboya said mildly.

"I see many difficulties."

"If the mosquito netting was still in place, then the killer could not have used the window to make his escape between the time you heard the shot and the time you woke up. If he used the door, and if as you say the shot is what woke you up, then it is hard to understand why you failed to notice him."

"If I were lying, I would have an explanation for that. As it is, I do not."

"Perhaps," Mboya said. "Tell me this: Why did you discard the pistol?"

"I did nothing of the kind."

"What did you do with it?"

"I spent a moment searching for it after the shot woke me up. I failed to find it and concluded that I had no more time to waste looking for it."

"Where was it when you went to sleep?"

"Under my pillow."

"Do you have anything else to tell me?"

That's always the wrap-up question for a *juge d'instruction*: *What you've given me is fine, but it's not enough; I want the rest.* Devereaux apparently had been through the drill before, and he didn't bite.

"That is everything I know."

"Thank you."

A good five minutes passed before Thomas and I were ushered back into Mboya's office, where there was no longer any sign of Devereaux. Mboya seemed remarkably calm for a civilian official who'd just been handed evidence that a senior field officer in his country's most elite army unit was guilty of murder, corruption, and something that sounded pretty close to treason.

"Well," he asked in English without turning around when he heard us come in, "what did you think?"

"It's nice to know my instincts were right," Thomas said. "He wasn't telling the truth to Sandy and me. Not the whole truth, anyway."

"Do you think he was telling the truth to me?"

"He would've been a fool not to. I don't think he's a fool."

136

"And yet, how was Hanson murdered if Devereaux did not murder him?" Mboya asked.

"I'm still working on that part of it," Thomas assured him.

"You have been involving yourself rather aggressively in the investigation of this matter, Monsieur Curry," Mboya said then.

"As I recall, my initial involvement wasn't at my own initiative. I seem to remember you pressing me into service." Mboya smiled.

"True enough. But I did not ask you to try to bluff Ndala into thinking you had information you did not have. I did not ask you to go to the French Embassy and create the impression that you'd learned something damaging there."

"You know Americans," Thomas sighed, raising his arms helplessly. "Once we get started, we just don't know where to stop."

"Now, of course," Mboya said thoughtfully, "you don't need to bluff anymore, do you? You actually do have hard information damaging to Major Ndala."

"Just a minute," I said firmly. I had no intention of letting Thomas get deputized again.

Both of them ignored me.

"Information harmful to Ndala isn't exactly a scarce commodity anymore though, is it?" Thomas asked.

"You and I know that," Mboya conceded. "But Ndala does not necessarily know it. I took some pains to be sure that my chat just now with Monsieur Devereaux will not become generally known."

"I see," Thomas said. "You have a political bombshell, but it's based on a dubious and unverifiable story from an adventurer trying to save his own skin. Ndala doesn't know you have it. But he probably suspects that I actually have some of the information Devereaux just gave you. Presumably, he also assumes that I have an acute desire to shake Burundi's dust from my feet as soon as possible. Given all this, you suspect that Ndala might have just enough rope to hang himself. That's your implication, isn't it?"

"Time will tell if I am right."

"Call your guards off me, let me wander around a bit on my own, and we might find out in a big hurry."

"Out of the question. The last thing my country needs at the moment is another dead American on our hands."

"Then what do you want from me?" Thomas asked.

"A prompt and complete report."

"About what?"

"About Major Ndala's next contact with you."

"I thought contacts like that were out of the question," Thomas said.

"Only on your initiative. You see, Monsieur Curry, you do not need to worry about stimulating any activity on Ndala's part. If I am right, he will find a way to get in touch with you."

"I'll cooperate cheerfully if you'll answer one question," Thomas said.

"That would depend on the question."

"Why were you going to Muramvya on the morning of the attack?"

Mboya paused for a moment before answering, gazing at Thomas in frank appraisal.

"I was going to arrest Alex Hanson," he said then.

"Then why didn't you do so as soon as you got there?"

"That is a second question, Monsieur Curry, but it deserves an answer nonetheless. You will recall that the only white at the inn when we arrived was ostensibly an Irishman with a passport identifying him as Terence Donoghue. I was looking for an American named Alex Hanson."

"Donoghue was obviously an assumed name."

"Obvious after the fact. On the face of the passport he'd left with the innkeeper, which I checked, everything appeared to be in order."

"Didn't you have a description of Hanson?" Thomas asked.

"Of course. We even had a somewhat dated photograph. Most important, though, we had a set of fingerprints."

"Then why the delay?" Thomas pressed.

"I wanted to match Hanson's fingerprints against the prints I expected the man calling himself Donoghue to leave on the photograph that I gave the inn proprietor to show him. Until I'd done so, I wasn't willing to risk arresting the wrong

138

man." Again he paused, making sure he had our attention. "A nation as young and poor as Burundi tries to avoid giving foreign countries reasons to throw their weight around."

I thought that Mboya glanced at me as he made that last comment—but maybe that was just my imagination.

27

"I am desolated by your disappointment, madame," the deeply tanned, gray-haired man behind the counter said to Sandy. Sandy was looking at his sharp-nosed profile, for he said this without turning his head toward her and without sounding particularly desolated. "But it cannot be helped. There is a war on."

"So I have heard," Sandy said dryly. "The war is to the north. I wish to be driven south, to Albertville."

"If the rebels were considerate enough always to be where they were supposed to be, the war would have been over six months ago—when it was supposed to have ended."

The filling station's tiny office stank of grease and fuel oil. Through its side window Sandy could glimpse the battered, chocolate brown 1953 Renault in which she hoped to be driven from Kasongo to Albertville, at the southern end of Lake Tanganyika. A sign on the Renault's windshield promised LICENSED CHAUFFEUR—DRIVING SERVICE.

A bored clerk at the airport had told her she'd find the Kasongo Deluxe Driving Service at this filling station, and

Sandy surmised that the Kasongo Deluxe Driving Service pretty much consisted of that Renault. The airport clerk had given Sandy this information after informing her that absolutely no flights, foreign or domestic, scheduled or charter, would be taking off from Kasongo until further notice. The airport clerk had also pointed out to her that there was a war on.

"I can pay you one hundred dollars, American," Sandy said to the man behind the counter. "That is probably more than the car is worth."

"It is at least twice what the car is worth, madame, but that is a matter of indifference. If the rebels or some trigger-happy Congolese troops shoot that car up while you are traveling to Albertville in it, I could not replace it here for a hundred American dollars—or a thousand, for that matter. Until things are quiet enough for the UN to pull out and the helicopters to stop flying, that car will stay where it is."

"Thank you for your help," Sandy said with uncharacteristic truculence as she stalked out of the office.

She told herself to calm down, to continue approaching the problem with system and method. A small, sharp rowel of panic nevertheless quickened her pace as she began walking the two-plus kilometers to the river. She had left Dray and Travis at the hotel café over an hour before. Dray must certainly have missed her by now.

From the first time she'd thought her plans through, she had realized that she'd have to improvise when she got to this stage. She kept reminding herself not to let her failure at the airport and then at the Kasongo Deluxe Driving Service upset her. But the fact remained that when she'd left Dray she'd had four options, and now she was down to two. And she didn't particularly like either of them.

Just over fifteen sweaty minutes later, Sandy spotted the ribbon of languid, green water and picked up the pungent smell of rotting fish that meant she'd reached the riverfront. She hurried toward the nearest group of wharfs, one bend of the river removed from the long row of warehouses where she and Dray had met Travis earlier that day. Nine damp stone steps, slick with tiny fish scales, brought her from street level to the part of the riverbank where the wharfs began.

Feeling slightly less pressured now, Sandy began to stroll along the wharf side, almost casual in her study of the small boats tied up to the pilings and the occasional knots of men laboring on them. She didn't know exactly what she was looking for, but she knew she'd find it. The dreary colonial endgame, with its lines of refugees, sporadic drama, and patina of tawdry anticlimax, had been woven into the fabric of her life from Indochina through Suez to Algeria. In every dying colony, savvy opportunists found some way to move ahead of the ebb and flow of battle. The Congo wouldn't be any exception. The rebels were about to lose, and people in Kasongo who'd backed them would be seeking discreet anonymity elsewhere.

Less than ten minutes later, Sandy spotted a light Fiat pickup chugging along the wharf road with a black, fifty-five-gallon oil drum taking up most of its cargo bay. She followed it with her eyes to the center pier, watched as it stopped there, waited as two men rolled the barrel from the truck down the lift-gate to the pier and then lowered it to a wooden, twenty-foot inboard motor boat riding gently there. When the Fiat had pulled away, she walked directly toward the boat.

Two black men were working on the deck. One, with a black-and-gray beard, had the engine hatch near the stern open and was fussing with the motor. The other, younger, clean shaven, missing the middle two fingers on his left hand, secured the oil drum amidships behind a barrier of truck tires cut in half and fastened like black crescent moons along the top of the hull.

Sandy sat cross-legged on the pier.

"Good afternoon," she said in French.

"Good afternoon, madame," the man amidships said, also in French, smiling broadly.

The man working on the engine grunted.

"How much for a ride to Albertville?" Sandy asked then.

The man amidships laughed.

"This is a fishing boat, madame," the man in the stern said. He examined oil that had spurted from the engine onto his forearm and swore under his breath.

"The fishing must be good near Albertville if you are taking on so much extra fuel," Sandy said. "Rationed fuel at that."

The younger man joined his colleague in the boat's stern, squatting beside him. The bearded man looked up at Sandy, his face expressionless.

"Six hundred French francs?" Sandy asked.

"The lady very much wants to get to Albertville," the younger man chuckled to the older one.

"We already have a passenger," the older one said.

"There is plenty of room," Sandy observed, her voice as unconcerned as she could make it. "Your passenger will not mind company, surely."

"If there are any armed Katangese left between here and Albertville, he may mind it very much, madame," the younger man said. "The rebels have unpleasant uses for women. Particularly European women."

"That is one of the reasons I am especially anxious to leave," Sandy said.

"Understandable." The younger man was still carrying the burden of the conversation from the boat. "But you must consider the problem from our viewpoint."

"One thousand French francs."

"We are dealing with a temptress," the younger man said jovially to his scowling companion. Then he looked back up at Sandy. "The fact remains that a boat carrying three men is just a boat, whereas a boat carrying a woman is a target."

"You have more courage than that," Sandy scoffed lightly.

"Did you hear that, my old friend?" the younger man demanded brightly, slapping his colleague on the chest with the back of his right hand.

"Yes, of course I heard it. And so?"

"If we take her, we will die. But if we leave her, we will be dishonored."

"Two hundred dollars," Sandy said. "American."

"Death or dishonor," the younger man said, stroking his chin in a parody of contemplation. "It is better that we take her." Swelling, baritone laughter rolled out of him.

"Very well," the older man said without enthusiasm. "Two hundred dollars American. In advance."

"Payment in full when we cast off," Sandy said. "If we cast off immediately, I will pay you immediately."

"Our other passenger will not be here for over an hour. We cannot leave until then."

Glancing at her watch, Sandy saw that it was just after 2:45.

"I will be back here in exactly one hour," she said. "Goodbye until then."

She moved briskly back toward the stone steps that led up to the street, vastly relieved that she wasn't heading for the warehouse to try to steal Dray's Landrover. That had been the fourth option, and now that it was unnecessary it seemed unthinkable in its improbability: talk her way into the warehouse; try to resurrect dim Algerian memories about how to start a jeep without the ignition key; pray that she could somehow get out of the warehouse with the Landrover; and then, having driven a four-wheel drive vehicle exactly twice before in her life, make her way to Albertville without much more idea of how to navigate than a vague hope that the main road would follow the river. Sandy shook her head, smiling briefly. *Faute de mieux* didn't begin to cover it.

Instead of undertaking that dubious enterprise, all she had to do was manage to avoid Dray for—she glanced again at her watch—fifty-four more minutes, until around 3:45, and then ride a motor boat to Albertville at 4:00.

It was curious, Sandy thought, how since her marriage her American assimilation had taken firm hold in some areas and skipped others. She still thought of distances in terms of meters and kilometers rather than feet and miles. But even two years before she wouldn't have said she was taking the boat at four o'clock in the afternoon—she would have said *seize heures*.

Seize heures.

Sandy stopped walking. She stood absolutely still.

Seize heures. Sixteen hours. In American military parlance, 1600 hours.

Which was when Travis had told Dray he was starting his own trip out of Kasongo. Not by plane, because no one was leaving by plane. Not by truck, because he had given his truck to Dray and said he was keeping only what he could carry. And not on foot unless he wanted to die young—besides which, if he were leaving on foot there would be no reason to tie his exit to any particular time.

That left the river. Coincidence was impossible. Travis had to be the other passenger on the boat that she'd just arranged for herself.

"I should be slapped for such stupidity," Sandy muttered to herself.

She turned toward the warehouses, by now nearly a kilometer away.

28

Sandy found a service door to the warehouse on the north side of the building, near its river end. After three series of increasingly impatient raps, an eye-level plywood square, like the judas door on a twenties speakeasy, snapped open. Sandy displayed her room key from the hotel to the hard brown eyes that appeared in the opening. She held the key so that only the top and the beginnings of the blade showed, hoping that that much of it would look something like an ignition key.

"Monsieur Dray sent me to pick up his Landrover," she said.

The square slammed shut. Eight agonizing seconds intervened before the entire door opened. The turbanned, brown-skinned man on the other side handed a clipboard and pen to Sandy, gesturing minimally at the signature line on a form attached to the clipboard. Sandy hurriedly wrote, "Laurent Dray, by Sandrine Cadette Curry" and handed it back to the man. Wordlessly, he stepped aside and let her in.

Sandy strode confidently across the echoing concrete. The warehouse was at least a hundred meters long. The Landrover was still parked next to the truck, around three-quarters of the way to the front.

So far so good, Sandy thought. *Now what?*

A Second World War–vintage American jeep had been part of the meager equipment available to her father's small command at the remote Algerian village where he'd served as *resident.* When the uprising began, he'd insisted that Sandy learn how to drive it, had made her take him out into the desert in it twice to be sure she could really do it.

That had been nine years ago. She hadn't driven anything since.

The jeep had had an ignition key, but the loyalist Algerians her father commanded seldom bothered to requisition it. Instead, they opened the jeep's hood and reached in with a long, rubber-handled screwdriver. She had watched occasionally as they'd touched the metal screwdriver blade to two leads or terminals or something on the engine block, causing the motor to turn over and start running. She closed her eyes and tried to summon back from deep in her memory a picture of the process.

Sandy reached the Landrover and climbed into the driver's seat. She didn't think the warehouse attendant was paying any attention to her, but she supposed she ought to make a show of trying what she'd passed off as the ignition key.

She gave that about three seconds. Then she began searching under the seats, in the back, in the glove compartment for a toolbox or an equipment pack or anything that gave some promise of holding a long screwdriver.

She came up empty. Dray must have been explicit in his instructions to the porters who'd come after his things. They'd apparently brought back to the hotel every portable object with any value at all.

Sandy climbed out of the Landrover, circled to its front, and fumbled the hood open, feeling clumsy and amateurish as she did so. The inside didn't look very much like her memory of the jeep. Just behind the radiator, though, on the front of the engine block itself, she saw what looked like they might be the two contact points that had to be put in circuit to start the motor. Now she needed something long and metal, and some way to insulate the part of it she was going to hold.

A bead of perspiration rolled from Sandy's forehead through her right eyebrow and then onto the lid and the lash where it blurred her vision for a moment. She brushed it irritably away.

Something long and metal. She thought of the hood brace and reached over to test it. As she did so, her eye fell on the radio antenna, mounted just in front of the hood, on the passenger-side fender.

She gripped the antenna appraisingly for a moment. Then, with a quick, decisive gesture, she snapped it off at the base.

With her eyes Sandy measured out a little better than a meter from the bottom of the metal rod. She broke it over her knee at that point, discarding its thin, whippy top.

Now for the insulation. France had used electrified fences in Algeria to cut up the vast spaces where the enemy could hide and move. Occasionally, Sandy had seen what was left of nationalists who'd learned about the fences the hard way. She wasn't going to overlook insulation.

Proceeding now with more assurance, Sandy moved to the back of the Landrover where a canvas-covered spare tire was mounted. This madly improvised plan of hers wasn't anywhere close to working yet—she couldn't even be sure that she'd actually found the right leads on the engine—but at least she now had a specific task to perform and that made her feel more comfortable.

She unzipped the spare tire's covering. Her thought had been to strip rubber haphazardly from the tire itself, but inside the tire's bottom she found something better: the long roll of patching rubber and tube of foul-smelling paste that Dray had used to patch a tire on the night before the ambush.

Fortune smiles at last, she thought absently. It took her less than a minute after she walked back to the front of the Landrover to wrap patching rubber around fifteen centimeters of the antenna's base and tie off the ends. If you liked broken, rubber-wrapped radio antennas, this was a good one. Now it was time to find out if she'd accomplished anything.

Tentatively, trembling just a bit with anticipation, she

148

extended the metal rod toward the gap in between the two leads.

Crack!

Startled, she stopped and looked up. The smack of the judas door snapping open reverberated like a pistol shot through the echoing, nearly empty warehouse. She didn't hear anything for several moments after that, but then the conversation at the service door got louder. Although she couldn't make out the words coming from outside the door, the voice was unmistakably urgent, unmistakably American—and unmistakably that of the man she'd identified as Kerry Travis that morning.

Sandy jerked the antenna out from under the Landrover's hood and lowered the hood flush with the chassis without slamming it shut. She ducked down between the Landrover and the truck, peeking over the hood toward the service door that the attendant hadn't yet opened.

There was an outside chance that Travis hadn't come down here looking for her—that he only wanted to get some of his own belongings out of the truck before his four o'clock boat ride. If that was the case, then hiding effectively in the back of the truck was a long shot, but hiding anywhere else was an impossibility. If Travis had come down here after her, on the other hand, then she was going to need a weapon. And the back of the truck was the only place she could think of offhand where she might find one.

Gripping the antenna, Sandy gathered up the remains of the puncture repair kit. She couldn't think of anything else lying around that might betray her presence. Awkwardly, she clambered under the blankets covering the truck behind her and into its bed. She winced as she scraped her shin on a rough edge inside the truck-bed's side wall.

Sandy's breathing came in shallow pants. Sweat stinking of exertion and dread saturated the armpits and back of her shirt. She couldn't risk lifting the covering blanket to look underneath it, but she had no trouble hearing the continuing, rancorous dialogue from the service door. It wouldn't take Travis long to figure out that a little money would get him farther with the attendant than a lot of shouting. She figured that she had thirty seconds to come up with a gun. If she were lucky.

She moved gingerly toward the back of the truck, to the crate that Travis had opened to show Dray. There had to be guns in there. Of that much she was certain. What else would Travis have been busily taking off the hands of Katangese rebels who figured the game was up? What else could qualify as heavy inventory being sold into a falling market? She didn't know whether they were pistols or rifles or machine guns, loaded or unloaded, but she didn't care. She was a soldier's daughter. Once she got some kind of firearm in her hands, she figured she could fake the rest.

Sandy pushed hard at the top of the crate. Travis had pried the nails loose this morning to show the contents to Dray, but they were sticking now, stubbornly resisting her efforts.

She heard the service door open.

With an explosion of breath she pressed upward with all her strength on the crate-top. Her left thumb split. Blood flowed carelessly over the splintered wood. But with a final protesting wrench the top came up.

Steps approached. Not quickly, but not casually either. Carefully. *He must know I am here,* Sandy thought.

Sandy reached into the crate for a gun. She winced. Not with pain. With bitter disappointment and sinking, nauseating fear.

The crate didn't hold guns. It held the only other valuable thing a beaten army has to sell, the last thing it sells before it gets rid of its guns and melts away: drugs and medical supplies. Bottles of quinine, jars of penicillin pills, sulfa, salt tablets, Merthiolate, snakebite kits, morphine. Nothing that looked like it would do much to equalize the fight with Travis that she now thought couldn't be more than ten seconds away.

"All right, frogette," Travis's voice called in English from what sounded like twenty meters away. "Come on up. I know you're back there."

He's not sure where I am, Sandy thought. *And he thinks I might be armed.*

As she retreated deeper into the truck, Sandy's hand fell on the antenna she'd rigged. A spark of an idea flared in her mind. One meter-plus of stiff, tempered metal. A long way from a rifle—but if there were only some way to give it a point it would be much better than nothing.

A point. Her mind was racing now. She felt five degrees cooler than she had a minute before. She reached back into the crate.

"We can do it the easy way or the hard way, frogette. Which is it gonna be?" The voice was no more than ten meters away now, and she hadn't heard the steps that had closed the distance.

Sandy fumbled in the crate through gauze, bandages, adhesive tape, aspirin. Then she found it—one of the snakebite kits. Pulling it out, she opened the small tin box: two suction cups; a leather thong; and a tiny lancet, no more than a curved section of razor blade with a thumb-size, round, metal base.

She fit the lancet base into the hollow top of the antenna. The opening was too big. The lancet sat loosely on top of the antenna.

"Okay, Genevieve or whatever your name is. Have it your way." Heavy boot steps drew inexorably closer.

Sandy smeared paste from the tire-puncture kit on a tab of rubber patch that she positioned over the opening in the antenna. She put the lancet base in the middle of the patch and shoved. The base slid into the antenna and held. The rubber patch wrapped around it as it went in, taking up the excess space.

Travis's hand brushed aside the blanket at the back of the truck. At the same instant, Sandy scrambled through the covering on the truck's other side and jumped to the floor.

In the moment it took Travis to dart around the back of the truck and confront her, she was on her feet. Her right toes pointed directly at Travis. Her left foot was perpendicular to her right heel, a shoulders' width behind it. Her knees flexed slightly, and her hips dropped a bit. She held the tipped antenna at perhaps a thirty-degree angle to the ground, the razor-sharp lancet at the end flicking slightly in response to almost imperceptible movements of her hand.

Travis stopped cold. He was wearing olive drab GI fatigues, the sleeves cut completely off the shirt to expose his muscular arms. He had a Colt Diamondback .357 magnum revolver in his right hand. That hand was still frozen in the position it had held when he'd caught sight of that flicking blade. The muzzle pointed about three feet to Sandy's left.

"You've got all kindsa spunk, sister, I'll give ya that. But the ballgame's over."

"Je crois que non."

"We're eight feet apart, right? You really think you can reach me with that overgrown toothpick and do some damage before I move my hand three inches and squeeze the trigger on this cannon I'm holding?"

"I am quite certain of it, monsieur. In fact, I am prepared to bet my life on it. The interesting question is whether you are willing to do the same."

Without the slightest suggestion of haste but without a speck of wasted motion either, her right foot stepped forward. Her left foot slid smoothly behind it. She straightened her arm, leveling the tipped antenna, as she began her next step.

Travis's eyes widened. He swung the gun muzzle toward Sandy. But he also backed up. It was impossible not to. Find a good fencer and try it sometime.

Step. Slide. The improvised sword slashed, not at the hand gripping the Colt but at Travis's face. I read somewhere that Caesar told his javelin throwers to try the same thing on Pompey's patrician troops during the Roman Civil War. It worked then, too.

The lancet bit into Travis's face just below his forehead and drew spurting blood from the bridge of his nose to his right cheekbone. In the moment's panic that gripped him as the blade sliced his skin, Travis backpedaled desperately and lost his footing. The revolver flew out of his hand and skidded across the floor as he landed on his back.

His discomfiture lasted less than a heartbeat. Recovering almost instantly, Travis sommersaulted backward and came to his feet, suddenly heedless of the wound that had distracted him a nearly fatal instant before.

He feinted toward the gun, lying five meters away. Sandy took the fake, hustling to put herself between him and the weapon. When she did that, Travis jumped in the opposite direction, darting in between the Landrover and the truck.

For a second Sandy hesitated, wondering whether to attack Travis immediately or try to retrieve the revolver. That

152

brief respite was all Travis needed. Opening the truck's door and reaching inside, he brought out a wide-bladed machete with a shimmering edge.

He turned triumphantly to face Sandy. The wound marring half his face made him seem more dangerous rather than less.

"Nice cutting, frogette. But I've been cut before."

Sandy resumed her original stance.

"If I had known that was in there," she said, nodding at the machete, "I could have saved myself a great deal of tedious improvisation."

"*Tant* the bloody *pis* for you, Joan of Arc. Now that I know what I'm up against, let's see how that toy of yours does against a real knife."

He came slowly toward her, slashing the air in front of him with heavy swings of the large blade. Sandy retreated, stepping now with her left foot, sliding her right, moving a shoulders' width each time. She took three steps back, kicking the gun farther away with the third.

Then, without warning, on the downstroke of one of Travis's air-shredding slashes, she attacked. She stepped forward with her right foot and leveled her sword. Travis reacted nimbly, moving into a smooth withdrawal.

Step. Slide. Step. Slide. Her advance continued, following his retreat.

Travis's machete swished viciously at her weapon. Sandy flicked the antenna out of the way. She stepped forward again, thrusting at Travis's right hip. He parried the stab, and Sandy had to pull her sword quickly down to the left to keep the machete's glancing, tinny contact from snapping her weapon in two.

Travis counterattacked with stunning speed as Sandy began an off-balance retreat. Sandy ducked. She swung the antenna up to block Travis's slash, but the oblique parry didn't come close to stopping Travis's heavier blade. The machete tip found her right shoulder, sliced through her shirt, and gashed the skin underneath. An instant's searing pain jolted through Sandy's upper body as she saw her own blood glistening on the edge of Travis's machete.

Sandy recovered her balance, backed up two strides, and

stopped. A different Algerian memory was coming back now, a memory not of mind but of instinct, soul, and spirit. Exhilaration, excitement, sheer joy gripped her. In an instant's epiphany, she understood exactly why Thomas had acted the way he had.

Travis paused, and that moment's indecision was enough for her. She attacked again. Step. Slide. Point. Step. Slide.

Then, as Travis re-placed his feet and waited for the next step, she didn't step. She exploded into a lunge, her left leg suddenly straightening, her right hungrily reaching over two strides' distance.

The lancet-tip started for Travis's groin. He jerked the machete clumsily down to block. The machete struck nothing but air as the lancet tip streaked around and up in an almost imperceptible semicircle, snaked inside the machete blade, and thrust sharply upward with force that started in the sole of Sandy's left foot and surged through her rigid right arm. The tip disappeared with eight centimeters of antenna metal into the right side of Travis's chest.

An expression of utter amazement washing over his face, Travis dropped the machete and clamped both hands to the wound. His mouth formed an O, but no sounds came out. He staggered backward and fell underneath the bumper of his own truck. Sandy's sword snapped as he did so, leaving her with a stub half the length of the original weapon.

She sensed Dray in the warehouse even before she heard his feet behind her scurrying toward Travis's gun. She didn't turn around. She stood still for a moment, transported, as the victory-rush coursed through her. The lancing throb in her own shoulder that she now began to feel in earnest actually seemed to enhance her elation. Breathing raggedly, she looked at the fallen man with bubbles of white-flecked blood coming out of the corners of his mouth.

"Madame!" Dray barked.

Still she didn't turn. She knew he had the gun, knew that it was trained on her spine.

"If you get him to a hospital quickly," she said over her shoulder, her voice nearly normal, "he may live."

"Madame, I will shoot," Dray called.

"Are you going to do it or talk about it?" Sandy said disgustedly.

She said it mostly to herself, scarcely loud enough for Dray to hear. As soon as the words were out of her mouth, she smiled bitingly at the comment's foolish, juvenile bravado. She didn't believe Dray was going to shoot, but she was dangerously close to not caring, any more than she cared much about the blood that had stained her sleeve and was now caking on her right shoulder. The combat glow still enveloped her. The intoxicating battle thrill buoyed her.

Turning slightly, she smiled at Dray. She tried to make the smile comradely rather than triumphant.

"For us the war is over," she said. *"Pour nous, la guerre c'est fini.* If you do fire, please try to finish me with one shot. As a professional courtesy."

Without lowering the revolver, Dray gazed at her, his face a mixture of wonder and longing.

"Are you proud of what you have done?" he asked.

Sandy thought about the reproachful query for a moment. It seemed like a fair question.

"Yes," she said. "I am not proud of enjoying it. But I am proud of having done it."

Dray dropped his arm, pointing the handgun's muzzle harmlessly toward the floor.

"Please tell me one thing, madame."

"If you wish," Sandy shrugged.

"Was I, if only for a moment, at least a temptation?"

"You deserve the truth, so that is what I will tell you," Sandy said. "I admire you. You are a competent and cultured man. But for me you were not even a near occasion of sin."

"It is a bitter thing to inspire admiration when one wants to excite passion."

Sandy's expression softened. Her smile glowed with the warmth of genuine affection.

"Of all seductions desire is the most deceitful," she said. "Whatever you want or.think you want, there is someone who already has it and is not happy."

Sandy swiveled away from Dray and walked toward the service door. Behind her she heard Dray scurrying across the floor to help the man she'd wounded, whose lungs were filling

155

with blood. Reaching the service door, she went out into sunshine. She stepped past the warehouse attendant who sat cross-legged against the outer wall of the building, studiously ignoring the events inside, his fingers occasionally tapping a wad of currency in the breast pocket of his khaki shirt.

It took her only ten more minutes to reach the boat that was waiting for her. With her left hand she motioned a request for the first-aid kit mounted on the inside of the stern.

"We can leave immediately," she said as she handed over the money she'd promised. "Your other passenger is not coming."

29

"So," Thomas said, "that's why I think I basically have it all figured out. Except for how they actually did it, I mean."

"Sure," I shrugged. "Except for how they actually did it. We can leave that part to the detail guys."

I glanced down at my plate on the pretense of polishing off the *crêpes avec de la glace* that I'd ordered for dessert. Thomas had just finished explaining his theory of the Hanson case, with Sandy's floor plan as the centerpiece. I should've been both attentive and impressed. I was neither. Instead of telling him how brilliant he was, I was tempted to suggest that he spend less time worrying about who'd killed whom and more time thinking about where his wife was and how to get her back.

I was trying as hard as I could to work up some genuine enthusiasm for Thomas's view of Sandy's absence, but I kept colliding head-on with the Enovid she'd picked up on her way out of Bujumbura. The rest of it I suppose you could work out some kind of rationalization for if you had enough imagination. But the birth control pills brought a kind of sleazy obviousness to the thing, didn't they? If they were a blind, whom were they supposed to fool? Dray, like most men, probably couldn't tell Enovid from Bufferin. A placebo would've faked him out if Sandy had thought fooling him were important. Sandy clearly had known one of Mboya's men was following her, but if buying birth control pills on a new prescription had told him anything it was that she was planning on slipping away—which was exactly what she didn't want him to know.

Well, I didn't say any of that. I just studied my plate, mopping up pancakes and ice cream with my fork.

We were in a private dining room at the Hotel Spaak's restaurant. The Hotel Spaak had insisted on this special treatment after Thomas acquired his rather intrusive retinue of Burundi cops. One of them, natty in a white jacket and white pith helmet, was standing right now at the room's doorway. When the waiter approached with brandy and snifters and the Diners Club chit for Thomas to sign, the cop stepped into his path.

First he examined the brandy bottle to make sure that the gold foil was intact and there was no evidence of tampering with the cork. Then, for the fourth time that night, he frisked the waiter. For the fourth time that night, he was briskly efficient and not particularly gentle about it. Only after he'd run through that entire routine did he let the hapless *garçon* approach our table.

Thomas studied the credit card form at some length while the waiter got the brandy open and approved by me—I was the one who'd chosen it—and then poured it into our snifters. Thomas signed the chit, tore off his carbon copy, and returned the rest of the form to the waiter.

"Thomas," I said, "I'm uncomfortable with where this thing's going. I didn't believe the private-citizen-getting-roped-into-international-intrigue business when I saw Jimmy Stewart doing it in *The Man Who Knew Too Much,* and Hitchcock was telling that story. Mboya's an impressive guy, but he's no Hitchcock."

"This brandy is first-rate, Theodore," Thomas said. "Well done."

"Thank you. Now—"

"I have no right to ask you to do what I'm about to ask

you to do," Thomas said then, his voice low and his tone conversational. "If you have the slightest reluctance about it, just say so, and we'll figure out some other way to handle the thing."

"You're waiting for me to feed you a straight line and I refuse to cooperate," I said.

Thomas responded by sliding the customer copy of the Diners Club chit across the white linen tablecloth toward me. I glanced warily at Thomas and tried to look sidelong at the chit at the same time, as if by staring at it directly I'd compromise myself.

"Now you've got me doing it," I said.

I picked up the paper and examined it. Hand printed in small, carefully formed letters on the white space underneath the credit card number was this message: "Madame Curry sends her compliments, and hopes that you will be able to send your *avocat* to the Cinema Pagnol for this evening's feature to receive further word of her."

This seemed to call for a reassessment of my opinion about what was going on.

"Looks like I'm going to the movies," I said.

"I thought it through while the waiter was fussing around," Thomas said. "They have to be trying to get a message through, don't you think? If they wanted a hostage, they'd have picked a less public place."

"Makes sense to me," I said dismissively.

"Now, if they try anything funny at all—if they tell you once you get to the movie house to proceed to some remote intersection or other unattractive venue, for example—don't fool around with it. Come straight back here. Understood?"

"I'm deeply complimented that you asked me to do this, Thomas," I said, smiling. "Don't spoil it."

I suppose it was God's idea of a joke that *North by Northwest* was that night's feature at the Cinema Pagnol. A real cosmic knee-slapper.

I took the note to mean that I was just supposed to go to the theater and wait for someone to get in touch with me. I went early, bought a ticket, and hung around the lobby for what seemed like a long time. I wished I could get a Coke or

159

some buttered popcorn or even some Milk Duds or Raisinets, but those commodities weren't available at the Cinema Pagnol. I finally figured that standing around the lobby wasn't getting me anywhere, so I went into the auditorium and sat in the back row.

An usher discreetly suggested that the view would be better from the second-last row on the theater's right wing. I took the hint.

The auditorium was big and gorgeously opulent in a way that made a virtue of excess, as movie theaters tended to be back then. Before the lights started to dim, I remember seeing lots of red velvet, gilt wood, and pastel silk. I suppose it should've been comfortingly redolent of normality, but my mood didn't lend itself to that kind of consolation.

As the credits began to roll, I let my mind wander over the theory Thomas had explained to me over dinner about the Hanson mess. It had an appealing internal coherence to it. It made sense. You had to suspend disbelief to accept the premise, but once you did that it all hung together. The major problem with it was the one Thomas had put his finger on: How had they done it?

On the screen, meanwhile, Cary Grant was already in serious trouble when a voice in the darkness behind me shook me out of my reverie.

"Monsieur Furst?"

"Yes," I answered after a startled shiver.

"Eyes front, if you please," the disembodied voice instructed me in French.

I obediently brought my head back to front and center. I don't claim to be good at accents, but I would've bet that French wasn't the first language this guy had learned to speak.

"You will if you please tell to Monsieur Curry the following points. One: Madame Curry is alive and well and anxious to see him again. Two: This reunion could come to happen very promptly after the trial of Devereaux is concluded. Three: If Monsieur Curry confines his testimony to matters he knows by his own observation—you understand? By his own observation, not by hearsay?"

"Yes."

"If he confines his testimony to these matters and avoids

speculation about other things, the trial is likely to end quite promptly indeed."

"All right," I said. "Now—"

"You will if you please be silent while I repeat these three points." He ran through it again, almost word for word except for the question.

"Understood?" he asked when he'd finished.

"Understood."

"You will if you please repeat the three points."

I was getting a little tired of the routine. I started to say, "Sandy's okay, and he'll see her again if he keeps his mouth shut." Fortunately, I realized in time that that'd just get me another five minutes of *"Répétez, s'il vous plait,"* and I ran through his message by the numbers instead.

"Bien," the voice said, as if I'd gotten the first declension right in a *lycée* Latin class. At least he didn't add *"pas de fautes."*

"Enjoy the rest of the movie," the voice instructed me then. "All of the rest of the movie."

I took that hint, too. I'm an accommodating kind of guy.

I was very impatient to get back to Thomas, but I sat there and forced my mind again over Thomas's exposition at dinner while Cary Grant and Eva Marie Saint exchanged smoldering glances. I'd just about gotten through it when Grant noticed something suspicious about a crop-duster biplane in the background.

He started to run. The plane swooped down and came after him. I'd seen the movie at least three times before, but I couldn't take my eyes off the screen.

Grant ducked a couple of efforts by the crop duster to clip him with its landing gear. Then things got serious. He ate dust as the biplane's machine gun hemstitched the Indiana prairie around him, kicking up dust geysers right behind his prone figure.

That's when it clicked. I continued to stare at the screen, but I wasn't watching *North by Northwest* anymore.

"Son of a gun," I said to myself. "So that's how they did it."

* * *

Mboya was with Thomas in his room at the Hotel Spaak when I got back there to report on my adventures. I probably shouldn't have been surprised, but I was.

"Intriguing," Mboya mused to Thomas when I'd finished my account of the message. "He does not ask for your silence. He asks instead that you testify about what you saw but not disclose what other people told you."

"Or what he thinks other people told me," Thomas said. "That eliminates any doubt about whether the message is from Ndala."

"I am going to bring Devereaux to trial, starting tomorrow," Mboya said. "I made that decision this afternoon, immediately after my interview with him."

"Tonight's episode makes your decision look pretty good," I said.

"My course was obvious," Mboya shrugged. "But your course, Monsieur Curry, is not so obvious. Is it?"

"Ndala's lying about having Sandy," Thomas said flatly. "I've seen his men in action. He has some people who could kill Sandy. But he doesn't have anyone who could take her alive."

I figured it wouldn't do any harm to take a really careful look at the toes of my shoes. They could've used a shine.

"*Bien,*" Mboya said. "I will see you in court tomorrow morning."

"You supply the questions," Thomas said. "And I'll provide the answers."

"I will look forward to it," Mboya said with finality as he rose to leave.

"There is one thing," Thomas added casually. "I'd appreciate it very much if you'd show me the picture as soon as it comes in from Sandy."

"What picture is that?" Mboya asked mildly. I was glad I wasn't the only one in the room who didn't know.

"I'm not sure," Thomas said. "But we'll know it when we see it, won't we?"

30

In every real trial I've ever seen, you spend a lot of time sitting around waiting for something to happen. That was the way it was when Claude Devereaux went on trial the next morning for murdering Alex Hanson.

An enormous teak carving of the Kingdom of Burundi's seal dominated the wall behind the judges' bench. The black silk, velvet-ribbed robes that the three judges wore reminded me more of European academic gowns than of American judicial garb. Their square, flat-topped black caps accentuated the impression. Seated in the middle, the presiding judge—the "president," in the French parlance that Burundi had adopted—had a lot of gray among the short, fuzzy hair that I could see under his cap. He looked to be in his early fifties, and he did all the talking on the panel. The other two, much younger, concentrated on taking notes and looking grave. Every twenty minutes or so, one of them would get carried away with excitement and nod soberly at something the presiding judge said.

There wasn't any jury, and there weren't as many spectators as I'd expected. Thomas and I and someone I guessed was monitoring the trial for the French Embassy were the only whites. Perhaps a dozen Watusi were scattered over the rest of the spectator section. Devereaux's lawyer scribbled assiduously with a fountain pen on unlined, onionskin paper clipped into a black leatherette folder. He didn't look like he was going to contribute very much to the proceedings. Every word that any of the principals said in open court was spoken in French.

Mboya seemed to dominate the courtroom. He strode confidently back and forth between the podium and counsel table, played with his own flowing black robe, snapped his fingers magisterially at the clerk who was supposed to distribute exhibits, and generally acted as if he owned the place.

Devereaux's trial began with a lengthy interrogation of the defendant himself, just as French trials did at the time. Mboya handled this as a matter of brisk routine, using Devereaux to describe the attack on the convoy and its aftermath and then letting him tell his story. In this heavily formal setting, the implausibility of Devereaux's version of events seemed even more glaring than it had in Mboya's office. I didn't have any trouble reading the judges as Devereaux finished his testimony and returned to the dock. They'd have hanged him right then and there if Mboya had asked them to.

Devereaux's testimony lasted an hour and a half. Mboya then called an assistant of his who spent a cozy fifteen minutes summarizing Mboya's reports about the condition of the body, the murder scene, and the surrounding area. I don't know if Burundi had a rule against hearsay evidence, but if it did Devereaux's lawyer didn't bother to invoke it.

When the assistant was finished, the presiding judge announced a ten-minute recess. Twenty-two minutes later we were still waiting for the trial to resume. During that interval, Mboya seemed a bit antsy, the way I used to when I was nervously waiting for a critical witness to show up.

The judges strolled back out around 11:15, and we got under way again. Mboya called Thomas to testify through an interpreter about what he'd seen during the attack and at Muramvya, and then what had happened to him later at Bujumbura. By the time he was ten minutes into the examination, I was sure my impression during the recess had been right: Mboya was stalling, deliberately trying to pad Thomas's testimony through to the noon hour so that he wouldn't have to go farther until he'd gotten whatever he was waiting for. Thomas was in the middle of describing the Watusi who'd relieved him of what turned out to be blank film shortly after he'd gotten back to Bujumbura when a tall black man marched into the courtroom holding two oversize brown envelopes. He handed one of them to Mboya's clerk. The clerk tendered it to Mboya. Without breaking his succession of carefully phrased questions or turning away from the podium, Mboya accepted the envelope, brought it to the podium, opened it, glanced at the contents, and nodded with obvious satisfaction. While that was going on, the messenger astonished me by retreating into the depths of the spectators' benches where I was sitting and handing the second envelope to me.

I thumbed it open and slipped out the eleven-by-fourteen-inch, black-and-white picture inside. It was one of the worst photographs I'd ever seen. The man and woman clinching with happy affection in the center were grossly overexposed, their features almost washed out. But the picture wasn't bad enough to keep me from recognizing Sandy hugging another man. I remembered Thomas's comment from the night before about the picture she was going to send. I felt as if someone had punched me in the stomach.

I glanced up as Mboya completed his examination of Thomas and paused to see if Devereaux's lawyer had any questions. He didn't.

"Would this be an appropriate time to break for dinner, Mr. President?" Mboya asked. "My next witness could not be here in less than a quarter-hour in any event."

"Perhaps so," the presiding judge said grudgingly, as if recessing with five minutes left in the morning were an immense concession. "Who will this next witness be, please?"

"Major Michel Ndala," Mboya said with quiet assurance.

31

"Major Ndala, allow me to begin by congratulating you on your unit's efficient repulse of the terrorist attack on a convoy going to Muramvya last week."

"Thank you," Ndala said in a brief, clipped voice.

Ndala looked magnificent standing in the witness box. He wasn't wearing a dress uniform but a garrison outfit: dark green blouse and pants set off by black combat boots, holster, belt, throat scarf, and beret. The boots, holster and belt gleamed with the glossiest shine I've ever seen on leather. Ndala stood erect but not rigid, stone faced but somehow radiating self-assurance, looking as if he'd been born to wear that uniform.

"As I recall, your helicopters appeared less than five minutes after the attack began."

"I am happy that we were able to respond promptly."

"By the way, Major," Mboya said then. "From what base did your troops leave that morning?"

"Lake Kasuba Cantonment."

"Some twenty minutes' flying time from the site of the attack, if I am not mistaken."

"Correct," Ndala said.

"From which it follows that your troops were in the air well before the attack began."

"Obviously."

"Which suggests, does it not, Major Ndala, that you knew about the attack in advance?"

"It could suggest any number of things." Ndala's face showed the suggestion of a smile that I assumed was intended to be disarming. "For example, it might mean nothing more than that we were on routine patrol."

"And the troops in your command who by great good fortune met the convoy outside Bujumbura and accompanied it the rest of the way—were they on routine patrol too, Major?"

"No." Ndala's smile disappeared.

"You had advanced knowledge of the attack, didn't you, Major?"

Ndala hesitated for a moment. I noticed a flicker of interest pass across the presiding judge's face.

"Yes," Ndala answered then. "We had reason to believe that an attack was threatened in that sector, and we took appropriate steps to thwart it."

"What was the source of this extremely useful information?"

"Military intelligence sources are confidential."

"Confidential?" the presiding judge interjected. "Just a moment—"

"If the court please, Mr. President," Mboya said. "I do not press the question."

Mboya had scarcely moved thus far during Ndala's examination. Now he stepped to the left side of the podium and rested his right hand on top of it.

"Perhaps you can tell me this, Major: The attack was highly unusual, was it not?"

"Terrorist attacks have fortunately been very rare in Burundi since independence," Ndala acknowledged.

"Particularly attacks by forces outside this country, correct?" Mboya asked.

"Yes."

"In fact, such attacks from Congolese terrorists have been unheard of, have they not?"

"That is perhaps an overstatement," Ndala said uncertainly.

"Major, can you think of a single one before the attack last week?"

"No," Ndala admitted after a long pause.

"Which of course is not the same thing as saying that Congolese forces have never been in Burundi—is it, Major?"

"I do not understand your question."

"You do not deny that Congolese rebels from Katanga Province have successfully hidden in Burundi at times over the past twelve months, do you, Major?"

"Anything is possible," Ndala said.

"You mean such a thing could have happened without your knowledge?" Mboya demanded.

"If we had known the whereabouts in Burundi of any foreign force, we would have treated them exactly as we treated the Katangese force last week."

"Well then, Major, let us return to last week's attack, shall we? How many enemy effectives were killed?"

"I believe the number was four."

"I am untutored in the military art, Major, but the number seems to me remarkably small in light of the overwhelming tactical superiority that you achieved."

"I wish it had been higher."

Abruptly, Mboya stretched out his right arm and snapped his fingers. The distinct crack sounded like a detonation in the suddenly quiet courtroom. Mboya's clerk, carrying what looked like a bulky poster, strode over to the side of the courtroom in between the witness stand and the tall, narrow windows. He flipped over what he was carrying to expose a thirty-by-forty-inch blowup of a photograph. He stood there like a human easel, holding the enlarged picture so that Mboya, the judges, and Ndala could all see it.

"Do you recognize this as depicting the scene of the terrorist attack on the Muramvya convoy?" Mboya asked.

"It could be," Ndala said after a brief glance at the enlargement. "I saw the site from a different angle, and I was somewhat busy at the time."

"Fair enough," Mboya conceded. "Then let's explore it together, shall we? You see four vehicles there on the road, such as were involved in the attack, right, Major?"

"There are four vehicles in the photograph, and there were four vehicles involved in the attack."

"And while it is a bit fuzzy, if you look closely in the foreground of the picture you can see at least three men in military clothing, off to one side of the road, who appear to be trying to conceal themselves."

"As you said," Ndala answered after a lengthier examination of the picture, "the photograph is very fuzzy."

"And then, Major, toward the right margin of the photograph as you look at it, there is another figure, is there not?"

Ndala studied the picture for several seconds. This time he clearly wasn't just going through the motions.

"Yes," he said then.

"The person appears to be white, wouldn't you say, Major?"

"It is hard to be certain, but he could be."

Without stirring or appearing to show any interest in what was going on, the presiding judge jumped into the dialogue.

"Let the record show that the figure referred to is clearly white," he said. "Major, I have no objection to your making Magistrate Mboya work for his information, but please do not make me work for mine."

"Of course, Mr. President."

"Will you agree with me, Major Ndala," Mboya resumed, "that this person appears to be moving away from the convoy, toward the area beside the road near the point where the attack came from?"

"His back appears to be toward the convoy, which suggests that if he was with the convoy at some point, he was moving away from it toward the attack sector at the moment the photograph was taken."

"Just so. And it is clear, is it not, that this picture was taken before the attack began?"

"Yes," Ndala said, his voice richly sarcastic. "The absence of smoke, fire, and twisted metal all suggest that."

"As if this person had left the convoy in the middle of nowhere with the idea of striking off on his own."

"If you please, Magistrate Mboya, I cannot read the mind of a blurry figure in a photograph."

"Do you know who Kerry Travis is, Major?"

"I do not."

"You were aware that Kerry Travis was supposedly accompanying the convoy, as a cargo handler on the truck in the rear?"

"I do not recall that specifically."

"And that Monsieur Travis was missing following the attack on the convoy?"

"I do remember that one white was listed as missing from the convoy, and Travis may have been his name."

"This tends to suggest that the fleeing white figure shown in the photograph is Kerry Travis, does it not, Major?"

"You are taking some liberties with the evidence, *Maître*," the presiding judge said to Mboya, using a somewhat affectionate, gently joshing diminuitive of "magistrate."

"In their very thorough search of the attack sector after the repulse of the terrorists," Mboya said briskly to Ndala, dropping the objectionable question, "did your men find any trace of Travis?"

"No."

"How do you account for this?"

"It was a combat situation. My men had other things on their minds."

"Did you know Alex Hanson before the murder?" Mboya asked.

"I knew that an American with that name was reported to be in the vicinity of Muramvya. I was not personally acquainted with him."

"Did you know him by sight?"

"No."

"Did you know what he was doing in and around Muramvya?"

"No."

"Did you know that he was trafficking on a regular basis with Katangese rebels encamped in Burundi?"

"I have just said that I did not know what he was doing."

"I thought the major's testimony a few minutes ago was that he also did not know of any Katangese terrorists present in Burundi," the presiding judge observed mildly as he paged through his notes.

"Thank you, Mr. President," Mboya said. "Major, you do not deny that Katangese rebels in fact had access to sanctuaries in Burundi from at least January of this year, if not before?"

"The assertion surprises me."

"But you cannot swear that it is false?"

"I suppose not."

"Knowing as you did that Alex Hanson was in or near Muramvya," Mboya said then, "had you taken any steps to obtain a physical description of him?"

"Not really," Ndala said.

"Allow me to show you another photograph, Major," Mboya said. "I regret, by the way, that because the picture was taken only yesterday and arrived at my chambers by wire only this morning, I have not had an opportunity to have poster-size prints made and can provide only conventional enlargements."

Without waiting for Mboya's finger snap, the clerk had put down the poster-size print he'd been holding and begun distributing eleven-by-fourteen-inch enlargements mounted on stiff, white backings to the three judges and Ndala. Thomas, sitting quietly beside me, pulled out our copy of the picture that had been given to me that morning while Thomas was testifying.

"Do you recognize the man in this picture, Major?" Mboya asked quietly.

"The picture is very poor so it is hard to be certain," Ndala said. "The man appears to be Laurent Dray, a Belgian national residing in Burundi. I believe he was picked up at one of my unit's checkpoints on the night of the murder in Muramvya."

"My apologies, Major," Mboya said. "I should have made my question clearer. I meant the man whose reflection appears in the window behind the couple in the foreground of the picture. If you look closely, you will see that that small part of the picture is well focused and properly exposed."

My eyes darted to our copy at the same instant Ndala's and the judges' did to theirs. I hadn't noticed it the first time. How often do you really notice anything in a photograph other than what looks like it's supposed to be the main subject?

171

Once Mboya mentioned the reflection, though, it jumped out at me. There in the window, just over Sandy's left shoulder, was the face of a bored, slightly irritated white male.

Ndala's reaction was unmistakable. For three very long seconds he stared at the picture, his mouth slightly open, his eyebrows knitted. I'd seen total surprise achieved in courtrooms occasionally before. I'd even done it once or twice myself before I figured out that I'd never get rich doing insurance defense work. Mboya had just achieved it.

"I do not know this man," Ndala mumbled after the pause.

"It is Alex Hanson, Major. Correct?"

"I do not—"

"After all, Major, Monsieur Devereaux can verify it, if no one else can."

"I do not know," Ndala insisted. "That is to say, I cannot be sure."

"You saw the body in Muramvya, did you not, Major?"

"Yes." Ndala seemed to have recovered some of his composure. A little starch came back into his voice. "I did see the body, briefly, in the dark and at some distance. But as I recall, the face had been blown away by the fatal shot."

"Correct," Mboya agreed. "And if, as I represented to the court a few moments ago, this picture was taken yesterday, we may surmise that this is not a picture of the person who was murdered in Muramvya following the terrorist attack. Are you with me so far, Major?"

"Obviously, it cannot be the same person," Ndala said.

"And if it is in fact a picture of Alex Hanson," Mboya said in a voice suddenly so quiet that we all unconsciously leaned forward, straining to hear it, "it would follow that Alex Hanson was not murdered in Muramvya, correct, Major?"

"Then who was?" the presiding judge demanded. I guess he figured he might as well jump in, as long as Ndala wasn't in any hurry to answer the question.

"Kerry Travis was murdered, wasn't he, Major?"

"I have no—I do not—"

"Kerry Travis was told that there was a profitable role available for him in a transaction with Katangese rebels if he

172

would meet them on the date of the attack, near that site, wasn't he, Major?"

No answer.

"He bribed his way onto the convoy and snuck away from it just before the terrorists struck, didn't he, Major?"

No answer.

"To his great surprise, however, he was rounded up by your men, wasn't he, Major?"

No answer.

"One of whom held his face a few inches from a pillow and by your orders shot him in the back of the head with an expanding bullet, didn't he, Major?"

"I know nothing of any of this."

"Then your men zipped Travis into a body bag as if he were one of the casualties from the attack and flew the body to Muramvya, while the rest of us waited at the attack site. That is what happened, is it not, Major?"

"This is absurd, and I protest being subjected to such—"

"The massive purplish discoloration around the victim's shoulders was caused by blood settling there while your men carried it upside down, wasn't it, Major?"

"I am a soldier, not a surgeon. I have no idea what you are talking about."

"I do, Major," the presiding judge said as he flipped back to his notes from that morning's testimony by Mboya's assistant.

"At Muramvya your men hid Travis's body in the wardrobe in Hanson's room, correct?"

"No," Ndala said sulkily.

"Later, after the rest of us arrived at Muramvya and Alex Hanson had been seen alive and well, one of your men gave Monsieur Devereaux the American .45-caliber pistol that had been used to kill Travis, correct?"

"That is Devereaux's story," Ndala said coldly. "Am I to understand that you seriously propose to accept the word of that white *canaille* over the testimony of an officer in the Burundi armed forces?"

"Unless you can confirm or deny some factual element in Magistrate Mboya's exposition, Major," the presiding judge said calmly, "please be silent."

"I deny the exposition altogether."

"When Devereaux joined Hanson in his room," Mboya said then, "Hanson gave him dried dates laced with a mild soporific, to be certain he would fall asleep well before midnight, correct?"

"I deny this." Ndala turned his head toward the court reporter. "Write that down. Write that I deny this."

"Then, Major, sometime before midnight, Hanson got up, made sure that Devereaux was sleeping soundly, took Travis's body and the pillow from the wardrobe, and planted them where they were eventually found, didn't he?"

"I will not answer this nonsense."

"The water on the floor was ice from the body bag in which Travis's body had been carried, was it not, Major?"

"Denied."

"Hanson left his own dentures on the bed stand, correct?"

"Denied."

"He found the .45 pistol that Devereaux had been given, correct?"

"Denied."

"He planted a small charge that could be electronically detonated on the windowsill, as in war cinemas, correct?"

"Denied."

"He took the body bag and left the room by its door, correct?"

"Denied."

Finger snap. The clerk was back in position between the witness stand and the windows. This time he was holding up a thirty-by-forty-inch version of the Muramvya floor plan. It looked a lot like the one Sandy had drawn.

"No one except you and your men saw him because he exited through the window in your room to the roof after you gave him Travis's passport and he gave you the .45, correct, Major?"

"Denied."

"After Hanson was well away, one of your men detonated the charge he had left in the room, correct?"

"Denied."

"Monsieur Devereaux was supposed to be killed 'resisting arrest,' but he refused to cooperate and succeeded in escaping from the room, correct?''

"Devereaux did escape from the room,'' Ndala conceded. "That is the first thing you have gotten right in ten minutes.''

"You had posted guards around the inn in anticipation of this possibility, hadn't you, Major?''

"I had posted guards because of a terrorist attack in the area that very day.''

"The guards were not there to keep terrorists out; they were there to kill Devereaux if he managed to get outside the building, were they not, Major?''

"Absolutely not.''

"You knew perfectly well that the terrorists were not going to attack Muramvya, did you not, Major?''

"I claim no such clairvoyance.''

"The only Katangese attack in Burundi was the one on the convoy that you had arranged through Hanson, correct, Major?''

"That is an outrageous charge,'' Ndala said hotly.

"It is an extremely grave charge,'' the presiding judge said. "Whether it is outrageous depends upon whether the magistrate has evidence to support it.''

"Hanson was the intermediary through whom you were accepting bribes to allow Katangese rebels to obtain sanctuary in Burundi from UN forces fighting them in the Congo, correct?''

"Denied. I was doing no such thing.''

"And when you learned that I was about to arrest him for smuggling and trafficking with foreign elements, you had to ensure that he escaped, right, Major?''

"Denied.''

"Because if he were arrested he would be tempted to expose your own activities, correct?''

"That is silly, in addition to being false. If that were my concern, I could simply have tipped him off and gotten him out of the country before you got to Muramvya.''

"No, you could not do that, Major, because in doing so you would have exposed yourself as the source of the revelation to Hanson that he was in danger of arrest—correct?''

"I was not—''

175

"The only effective way to protect yourself was to close my investigation by having Hanson die or at least appear to die, right, Major?"

"You are fantasizing."

"To avoid casting suspicion on yourself, you needed to frame someone for the murder, and for that you needed Hanson's cooperation, correct?"

"Nonsense."

"Which was unlikely to be secured unless some way could be found to leave him alive at the end of the operation, correct?"

"I did not require any cooperation from this person I never knew."

"That is why you seized upon Monsieur Travis as a convenient victim, right, Major?"

"Denied."

"Magistrate Mboya," the presiding judge said, "what evidence, precisely, do you have to support this intriguing theory?"

"For the most part, Mr. President, the evidence is already before the court. Alex Hanson, without dispute, was alive and well in a room occupied by him and Devereaux the afternoon and evening following the terrorist attack on the convoy. By the small hours of the following morning, that room was occupied not by Hanson and Devereaux but by Devereaux and the body of someone other than Hanson. Hanson had meanwhile escaped from an inn under airtight surveillance. This entire turn of events could only have come about with Major Ndala's active collaboration. Therefore, Monsieur Devereaux's tale of culpable transactions between Major Ndala and Katangese rebels, however implausible it may appear on its face, is supported by a body of objective and irrefutable evidence."

"Q.E.D., *Maître?*" the presiding judge asked with a grim smile.

"Q.E.D., Mr. President."

"Well and good. But your entire theory depends on the premise that the photograph of Hanson's reflection was taken yesterday, rather than several weeks or months ago."

"I agree, Mr. President."

"Do you have any competent proof that that is the case?"

"Yes, Mr. President. Tomorrow morning, I will be in a position to present the testimony of the young woman shown in the picture, who can verify that it was taken yesterday in Kasongo, in the Congo."

"Major Ndala," the presiding judge said then in the same dispassionate tone, "you will, if you please, deliver your side arm to the bailiff and report to the Criminal Bureau of the *Palais de Justice* to await the instructions of Magistrate Mboya."

32

"I will do nothing of the sort," Ndala spat.

He stepped from the witness stand, wheeled around with parade-ground precision, and moved briskly toward a door in the rear corner of the courtroom. Springing forward, the bailiff clamped his right hand on Ndala's left shoulder.

Ndala stopped. He turned his head almost nonchalantly toward the bailiff. Chilly contempt played unambiguously across his face as he gazed steadily at the civilian. For a moment the bailiff just stood there, as if he had no idea what to do next. Then he held out his left hand, palm up, to receive the surrender of Ndala's pistol. In Kirundi, French, or English, the expression on Ndala's face said, *Who do you think you're kidding?*

Ndala held the bailiff's eyes with his own for perhaps five seconds, long enough to let the bailiff think things over, think about whether he really wanted to try to take a pistol away from an Army officer with a combat command. It seemed to me that it wasn't fear Ndala was trying to awaken in the bailiff so much as a sense of unthinkability: *This just couldn't happen, and it isn't going to happen.* Then he jerked free of the bailiff's grip with one powerful stride and reached the door with another. When the bailiff finally jumped forward after a moment's frozen hesitation, he was too late. The door slammed in his face after Ndala went through it.

Thomas bolted from our bench in the spectator section, vaulted the railing, and sprinted toward the back door. The presiding judge had already hustled spryly from the bench and was grabbing a telephone on the table in front of it. The bailiff was rattling the door as if trying to get past a bolt Ndala had thrown on the other side of it, but I can't say he was proceeding with a great deal of enthusiasm.

Reaching the door, Thomas slammed his shoulder into it. I heard something splinter, but from my distance I couldn't be sure whether it was wood or bone. Thomas was just about to take a second crack at the door when Mboya spoke.

"Wait," he said in English.

He had sauntered over to the window side of the courtroom, and he issued this instruction while leaning against the sill. Thomas and the presiding judge both gaped at him.

"What do you mean 'wait'?" Thomas demanded. "You just guaranteed that that brass hat's going to put killing Sandy at the top of tonight's priority list."

"An excellent reason to keep from getting yourself killed this afternoon, *d'accord?*" Mboya responded mildly.

"What do you mean?"

Mboya jerked his head toward the window. Thomas and I darted for it at the same time. I was closer and he was faster. We arrived together.

Soldiers in helmets and combat fatigues were pouring out of a canvas-covered truck pulled up on the plaza that surrounded the building we were in. In a column of twos, their rifles at port arms, they double-timed toward a side entrance three floors beneath us.

My gut got chilly all over again. There were only twelve of them, though it seemed at first like more. One dozen or six dozen, it didn't make much difference. They clearly meant business, and whatever collection of cops and building security officers the Bujumbura *Palais de Justice* could scrape up wasn't going to keep them from taking Ndala out with them.

179

Implicitly conceding as much, the presiding judge put down the telephone.

"Presumably," Mboya said, "Ndala signaled them from the stairwell window. He had them in place in advance. He knew exactly what he was going to do if my questions became ah, excessively provocative."

"Excellent analysis," Thomas said. "Really first-rate and all that. *Mais je ne m'en fiche pas.* I want to know where Sandy is, and I want to know right now."

"I suggest that we discuss this question in a less public venue," Mboya said, quite calmly.

"At the moment," Mboya said after glancing at his watch ten minutes later in his office, "Madame Curry is at the French Consulate in Albertville, Katanga Province, the Congo. At approximately thirty minutes before dusk this evening, she will be on a Congolese patrol cutter flying the UN flag and crewed by Belgian marines. The cutter will be as close to the center of Lake Tanganyika as it can get without leaving Congolese territorial waters. There, she will be met by the only helicopter owned by Burundi's Judicial Police."

"Forgive my skepticism," Thomas said acidly. "But from what Theodore explained to me of the testimony this afternoon, the Burundi Judicial Police leak like a sieve—especially to Ndala. Before the sun's over the yardarm this evening, he'll know enough to blow that copter out of the air."

"This possibility was not entirely unanticipated," Mboya said. "By emergency royal decree promulgated over the noon hour, all other Burundi aircraft—military, civilian, and police—will be grounded from two hours before the helicopter takes off until forty-five minutes after it lands at Bujumbura."

"I have a better idea," Thomas said. "Why don't we just leave Sandy in Albertville? If her testimony is so important, you can take it there."

"You have convinced me," Mboya shrugged. "I suggested something along those lines to Madame Curry already. She seemed to attach considerable importance to coming back to Bujumbura herself."

With that comment, Mboya achieved the distinction of

becoming the only person other than Sandy herself to shut Thomas up, even briefly.

"Ndala must consider his options carefully," Mboya said. "He has compromised himself by his behavior this afternoon. The most prudent course will be for him to slip through our fingers—take what he can and flee Burundi."

"That's really what you're hoping he'll do, isn't it?" I asked.

Mboya shrugged.

"The rule of law in Burundi is still fragile," he said. "It is not yet ready for a frontal test of strength with the army. It must prevail by finesse rather than by raw strength."

"But what if Ndala doesn't take the prudent course?" I pressed. "What if instead of twelve airborne troops, it's twelve hundred? And what if instead of marching on this courthouse, they're marching on the royal palace?"

"From the midpoint of Lake Tanganyika," Mboya said, "I suppose a helicopter could fly west as easily as east."

I nodded.

"You'll be on the helicopter?" Thomas asked Mboya.

"Yes."

"So will I."

I winced at this undiplomatic Yankee assertiveness, but Mboya seemed unperturbed.

"Yes, I rather hope you will," he said. "As I said before, the last thing Burundi needs right now is another dead American."

33

The seat belt's click as I buckled it across my stomach seemed solid enough, but somehow it didn't reassure me. I'd never been on a helicopter before, and I'd already decided to make this first experience my last one. The craft's long, skinny passenger space featured sheet metal, exposed bolts, and the sweetly nauseating stench of gasoline.

"I'm still not sure why I'm along on this trip," I said to Thomas. "My draft classification is 'hostage.' "

"You're along for the same reason I am," Thomas said as he craned his head around to watch Mboya's approach through the open hatch. "If armored personnel carriers start rolling through Bujumbura tonight, Mboya wants to make sure you're hightailing it for Albertville along with the rest of us."

Mboya clambered onto the helicopter and lurched into a seat across the narrow aisle from Thomas. As a ground crewman swung the hatch shut, the air inside suddenly seemed claustrophobically stale and close. It was like being in a Volkswagen Beetle with a leaky carburetor and the windows closed in August.

"Everything clear?" Thomas asked Mboya.

"The radio reports that no other aircraft are flying in Burundi airspace," Mboya said, nodding.

"They could be waiting until they know we have Sandy on board," I said.

"Theodore's middle name is Pollyanna," Thomas told Mboya.

"No one knows when we will have her, where we will pick her up, or where we will take her," Mboya said, raising his voice as the engine revved. "I am the only person in the country who knows exactly where this helicopter is going to fly. I will not even give the pilot his instructions until we are in the air."

"You may find it comforting to keep your eyes on that, Theodore," Thomas said, pointing at a white bundle about the size of a lumpy backpack wedged directly behind the pilot's seat. "It's a parachute. You don't often see them on helicopters."

"I don't have much practice with parachutes," I said.

"That's okay. As my first flight instructor told me when I asked about parachute training, there's no sense practicing something you have to do right the first time."

The craft lifted off the ground and my stomach followed about three seconds behind everything else. When we reached three hundred feet or so, Mboya took a sheet of flight-plan instructions from his inside coat pocket and edged forward through the cabin until he could give it to the pilot. I thought I saw a flicker of curiosity in Thomas's eyes as the pilot swiveled around to accept the page, but at the moment I had neither the physical ability nor the psychological inclination to ask him about it.

We flew straight for the setting sun and found ourselves over the immensity of Lake Tanganyika within a couple of minutes. From the air the water looked sparkling blue, especially as we moved away from the shore. Not that I spent much time enjoying the view. I concentrated on keeping my lunch down.

Thomas, as he explained to me later, concentrated on Ndala. He tried to put himself in Ndala's place, to figure out

183

how Ndala would think through his options and what approach he'd develop to get out of the fix he was in.

Half an hour or so into the flight we were well out over the lake with nothing but sun and water between us and the horizon in any direction. It seemed to me that we had to be pretty close to the halfway point by then, but we still had to buzz around in gut-twisting little circles for a good ten minutes before we spotted the cutter with its white-on-blue flag snapping in the breeze.

As we swooped down, I risked a look. A glimpse of Sandy standing on the deck near the stern and waving enthusiastically rewarded me.

She looked like death warmed over. Her hair was ragged, her face and arms scratched and bitten, and an awkward bandage bulged on her right shoulder. Even viewed from twenty-five feet above the ship, though, her smile more than made up for all of that. Hanson's reflection in the picture Sandy had wired from Albertville had analytically refuted my doubts about her disappearance. Seeing Sandy in the flesh made those doubts seem so absurd that I wondered if I'd ever really entertained them.

I'm told there are three ship movements sailors worry about: pitch, yaw, and roll. I don't know which is which, but I'm pretty sure the cutter did all three of them several times while the copter was landing on its deck. Landing a helicopter smoothly and safely on level ground isn't any feat to be sneezed at. Landing it on two hundred square feet of wood and steel that's listing thirty degrees to starboard one minute and twenty degrees to port the next is a lot more challenging. The pilot managed it, but there were several bumps and jolts in the process that had my belly and my throat in uneasy proximity.

Before the helicopter skids were secure, Thomas was out the hatch and sprinting nimbly along the deck to meet Sandy, who was hurrying just as anxiously toward him. They met in a clinch worthy of the first Patterson/Johanson fight. Sandy lifted her heels in the air as Thomas pulled her off her feet and swung her around in a fierce, almost desperate embrace. Her fingernails dug into his back as he kissed her hungrily on the mouth and the throat and the neck. Laughing and crying at the same time, Sandy laid her face contentedly on Thomas's chest.

I watched the whole thing. As long as I'd paid for the ticket, I was going to see the show. I gave it a rave review. If it had been in a theater I would've walked out whistling the score.

Thomas and Sandy had plenty of time to get reacquainted because it took quite a while for Mboya and the top civilian official on the ship to satisfy themselves that they had the paperwork straight and it was all right for Mboya to fly off with Sandy. They finally got it done. I'd describe it in more detail, but most of the time they were at it I was busy at the rail being sick.

Night had fallen and complete dark enveloped the ship when we finally climbed back in the helicopter to take off. Mboya sat in the copilot's seat for the return trip so that he could stay in touch with Bujumbura by radio. Thomas and Sandy sat together, in the part of the passenger cabin directly behind Mboya. They made it clear that they were immensely pleased with each other's company.

I buckled myself into a hard, metal seat, wedged my right hip against the fire extinguisher fastened to the bulkhead, and put my head between my knees. Cold sweat popped out on my forehead as we lifted off, but I ignored it. Eyes squeezed shut, I tried to figure out what it was that was bothering me about the inside of the helicopter.

The copter only had a couple of dim dome lights in the passenger cabin. I raised my head and let my eyes get used to the semidarkness. An amber glow came from the instrument panel in the cockpit. After we were airborne, the pilot flipped a switch and several of the instrument readings flashed directly onto the windshield in luminous green. These were clearly visible from the passenger cabin, and I thought I saw Thomas look sharply at them with what seemed like more than casual interest.

Mboya chatted calmly on the radio for less than a minute. He cut off the conversation before anyone could possibly have used the transmission to get a fix on our position.

With some irritation at my own slowness, I asked myself what was wrong. Mboya's preparations seemed foolproof. Neither Ndala nor anyone else inside Burundi could possibly know where we were. Even if they did, they wouldn't have any way to attack us as long as all aircraft in the country were grounded. I couldn't see any flaw. Why did I have this nagging sense that I was missing something?

The helicopter throbbed through the night. Forty minutes or so slipped past as we plowed through a dark void without any real sense of either forward motion or passing time.

I shivered a bit. We were flying higher than we had on the way out—high enough that even the tropical air turned chilly. Pulling my lightweight suit coat tighter, I buried my fingers under my armpits.

"It looks like he's going to take us into Bujumbura through the backdoor," Thomas said to Sandy several minutes later, pointing at the green numbers on the windshield. "He's set the course for well north of the city."

Following his finger, I looked at the copter's windshield myself. I saw the first faint glint of lights in the distance. *Thank God,* I thought to myself. *It can't be much longer now.*

Closing my eyes, I counted silently to one hundred and fifty. Then I looked at the windshield again, to see how much closer the lights had gotten.

Through the glass I could now see two symmetrical rows of white ground lights burning through the night perhaps a mile away. That's when it came to me. I think Thomas realized it at the same instant.

"Thomas!" I yelled. "The parachute's gone!"

The pilot jerked around at the sound of my raised voice. Thomas smiled coldly at the sight of the man's face.

"Hello, slick," Thomas said.

Then Thomas's right foot snapped out and up across the aisle and kicked the man in the teeth.

The pilot's head whiplashed violently backward as his hands flew from the controls. It took Thomas less than half a second to unfasten his seat belt, but that was enough time for the pilot to recover, free himself from his own belt, and charge out of his seat at Thomas, who was hurrying to his feet.

The helicopter lurched sickeningly downward and to the left. I saw Sandy's face go white with pain as the lurch slammed her wounded shoulder against the bulkhead. The helicopter continued its pitching swerves as its autogiro tried valiantly to stabilize it.

186

The pilot smashed his head full force against Thomas's face, as if he were trying to head a soccer ball into the goal. Thomas crashed to the floor with the pilot on top of him, the pilot's hands groping for Thomas's throat. Thomas flailed with his fists at the pilot's kidneys, but his punches fell harmlessly on the parachute that the pilot had slipped on while the rest of us were fooling around on the cutter's deck. The helicopter plummeted in tight spirals as an ominous engine whine filled the cabin. My stomach sloshed acid that I tasted on the back of tongue, my diaphragm turned to jelly, and I felt as if a giant, splayed hand were pressing me against the bulkhead.

All this took less than two seconds, and in a fraction of that interval my own synapses flashed a grim syllogism through my brain:

(1) The pilot was the disguised soldier who'd relieved Thomas of his decoy film several days ago. Under Ndala's orders he'd somehow contrived to replace the Bujumbura Judicial Police pilot who was supposed to be flying the copter;

(2) He'd taken the copter to a thousand feet so that when we reached the temporary landing field marked out ahead of us he could bail out, leaving us to crash or, failing that, be brought down by ground fire;

(3) He was now in a death struggle with the only other person on board who could fly a helicopter, while Sandy was disabled with pain and Mboya was strapped into his copilot's seat like a giant, useless, upended turtle, unable to fly the helicopter at all and unable to do anything anytime soon;

(4) Meanwhile, the helicopter was losing altitude at over a hundred feet per second;

(5) Therefore, we were all going to die unless Theodore Furst did something in a big hurry.

Looking back on it, I'm not sure I actually saw the altimeter readings flashing on the windshield over the next six seconds, but I still get nightmares about this experience and, when I do, those same green numbers are there, every single time.

760. I yanked the red steel fire extinguisher from its bracket on the bulkhead beside me and pointed its black cone at the pilot.

625. After fumbling once, I mashed the trigger and sent

a jet of white chemical foam spraying directly into the pilot's face. He jerked his beefy hands from Thomas's neck and pawed frantically at his eyes.

465. Thomas freed his arms, brought both hands straight up in the air, and delivered a massive double rabbit punch to the back of the pilot's neck. The pilot's body went limp for a moment. Thomas scrambled out from under him.

290. Those ground lights that had seemed so far away now looked like some drunk's headlights screaming at us on the wrong side of the freeway. Thomas pulled himself feverishly over the pilot's prone body as if it were a gangplank. I raised the fire extinguisher to smash its base on the pilot's head, but I'm just not cut out to be a killer. I flinched at the last moment and landed a glancing blow that probably wasn't good for much more than an Excedrin headache.

120. Thomas reached the cockpit and grabbed at the controls. Removing the military-style webbed belt from her trousers, Sandy staggered forward and planted her knee in the center of the pilot's parachute. She looped the belt around the pilot's neck, threaded the free end through the buckle and pulled it tight. The pilot had recovered from my feeble assault and was starting to move his arms, but when the belt took hold he stopped quick.

80. Thomas got control of the copter. The high-pitched whine stopped, and the suddenly reassuring roar of the engine and alternating chop of the rotor resumed.

We were directly over the lighted landing field now, and Thomas continued to drive the copter down. He'd realized that the troops there weren't going to shoot at us as long as they thought we were going to crash. The instant he pulled the copter out of its dive, they'd try to blow us apart.

Maybe I only imagined distinctly seeing a cigarette butt on the earth in the ground-light glow before Thomas finally yanked the joystick into his gut and jerked the copter skyward. I swear the landing skids kissed leafy treetops as we cleared the end of the field. Small arms and machine gun fire crackled behind us, but by the time we pulled up we were so far east that they had to swing their big guns around to aim at us. Before they could do that it was too late. All the copter had to show from the groundfire was a couple of pinged struts.

Sandy looked pretty wobbly to me, and I couldn't blame her.

"I can take that," I said, reaching for the belt end.

"Thank you," she murmured as she relinquished it to me. Then another spasm of pain from her shoulder jolted her, and she passed out.

Mboya by this point was talking rapidly into the radio microphone. His first conversation was in Kirundi. I didn't understand it, but from his tone I gathered that the guy on the other end wasn't saying anything but how high, how fast, and what color. There was a pause during which he must've moved up the ladder, because his next words were in French.

"I wish to speak directly to the premier, and I wish to do so immediately, if you please. . . . I do not care whether he is in bed or in his bath, alone or with company. I insist on speaking to him directly and without delay. . . . Mboya here. Troops under the command of Major Michel Ndala knowingly and intentionally fired tonight on what they knew to be an aircraft of the Bujumbura Judicial Police. Ndala has taken an irrevocable step. If you do not find some loyal soldiers and place him under arrest in the next two hours, you might as well hand him the keys to the palace. Give some orders and see to it that they are faithfully executed. . . . I do not know the exact location, but it took place on the coast some considerable distance north of Bujumbura. . . . Of course I know it happened. I was there. . . . Right. Mboya out."

"You do realize, of course," Thomas said, "that anyone in Burundi with a short wave receiver could have listened in on that conversation?"

"The basic principles of radio transmission are not a complete mystery to me, Monsieur Curry."

"So you have to assume that Ndala will know every word you said within five minutes."

"I not only assume that, I am counting on it."

"Don't you think he might run instead of waiting around to be arrested?" Thomas asked.

"Yes, I rather think he will. I very much hope that he is on his way north or west right now. Once he flees he will lose the support of his men, and an officer who is either more honest or less clumsy can replace him in command of the north-central military district."

Mboya had unbuckled his seat belt and taken the first-aid kit from under his seat. Extricating himself laboriously, he felt his way into the head of the passage where Sandy lay. He removed his coat and slipped it under her head, then began sponging her forehead with gauze.

"What if Ndala decides to take a stab at running Burundi himself instead of taking off?" I asked.

"I do not think he will," Mboya said. "If he felt he were strong enough for that, he would have concentrated his troops in Bujumbura and done it instead of diverting part of them to the north for that ambush."

"What if you're wrong?"

Mboya glanced around at me, smiling, as he broke a capsule of smelling salts under Sandy's nose.

"If I am wrong," he said serenely, "we should be made aware of it shortly after we land."

Tightening my grip on the belt, I looked at Mboya with different eyes. It wasn't just dry wit or bravado. He really meant it. The die was cast. The trial didn't matter, Devereaux didn't matter, none of us in the helicopter mattered anymore. We'd all been just means to an end. It was law versus force in Burundi. Issue was joined, and we'd see who won.

"So whichever way it comes out," I said, "you've done your job."

"I am pleased to think so."

"Even if it gets all of us killed?"

"As your own General Sherman put it," Mboya said placidly, " 'war is hell.' "

"So it is, *Maître*," Thomas said over his shoulder with an explosion of laughter. "So it is."

There was a touch of hysteria coloring the laughter, but only a touch. If I'd trusted myself to laugh, there would've been a lot more.

34

Devereaux didn't come to see us off. I can't say I really minded. It would've spoiled things a bit if he had. He'd been acquitted of Alex Hanson's murder on the technicalities that Hanson hadn't died and Devereaux hadn't killed him. Apart from that, there was no really persuasive argument against conviction.

Mboya did join us at Bujumbura International Airport three days after our dramatic helicopter ride while we waited for the flight that would take us to Leopoldville. As Mboya had predicted, Ndala had picked up Mboya's radio message and had been on his way out of Burundi before our helicopter landed. He had escaped, but by running he'd lost the loyalty of his troops and that meant he was through in Burundi for good.

"What about Dray?" Thomas asked Mboya. I was glad he did. It was an interesting question, and I sure wasn't about to bring it up.

"I understand that he has made some discreet contacts in an effort to find out what the government's attitude might be if he should return," Mboya said.

191

"I'd think the answer would be short and unambiguous," I commented. "He apparently was using his guide business as a front to collaborate with Hanson and Ndala in contraband trafficking, border jumping, and treason."

"It is not my decision," Mboya shrugged. "What you say is just. On the other hand, people such as Dray serve useful functions in a small country like Burundi."

"Perhaps so," I conceded. "Put Dray and Devereaux in the same bar around closing time, and justice may be done after all."

Mboya smiled tolerantly.

"Monsieur Furst, when I was a young *avocat,* matched repeatedly against more experienced *procureurs,* I lost a lot of cases that I should have won. Later on, as I gained experience and came more frequently to be opposed by younger counsel less skillful than I, I won a lot of cases that I should have lost. So you see that, in the end, justice was done. In the end, justice is always done."

A tinny voice on the public address system interrupted the brief silence that followed by summoning "Madame Coo-ree" to the information desk for a telephone call. Mboya offered to show Sandy where that desk was, which left Thomas and me alone for a few minutes.

"You've figured most of it out for yourself already, haven't you?" Thomas asked quietly.

"I think so. Sandy bought a new camera because if she'd taken the Pentax, Hanson would've been looking directly through the lens while he took the picture. His face wouldn't have been reflected in the window, and he could've seen that the camera wasn't really set to take a picture of Sandy and Dray. And Sandy saw the priest before she left with Dray so she could go to confession, because she knew there was a good chance she'd be killed before the trip was over."

"But you still haven't figured out the birth control pills, have you?"

"No," I conceded.

"It's a common failing with you Catholics, Theodore."

"Lapsed Catholics, in my case," I said.

"Lapsed Catholics, in your case," Thomas agreed. "You know the rules of your religion the way most Americans know the rules of English grammar. You're very solid on the general principles, but you're a bit unsteady on the details."

"Thomas, you have achieved perfect opacity. What in the world are you talking about?"

"The Catholic Church doesn't forbid people to take birth control pills. It forbids people to have sex after they've taken them."

"Thank you for explaining that arcane and, I'm sure, highly pertinent distinction," I said.

"If a Catholic woman has no intention of being sexually active in the first place, the Church sees nothing wrong with her taking birth control pills for some other reason," Thomas explained with elaborate patience. I still wasn't getting it, so he spelled it out. "For example, the Church itself distributed birth control pills to nuns in the Congo missions—when it became clear they were in danger of being raped by Katangese rebels."

Oh. Now I got it.

"I mention that," Thomas said as he saw Sandy and Mboya about thirty feet away, coming back from the information desk, "only because I knew it would drive you crazy not to have the last piece of the puzzle—and because I never want to discuss what happened in Burundi again."

"Understood."

"That was Devereaux," Sandy said as she reached us. Her luminous smile accented the playful sparkle in her eyes. "He wanted to say thank you—and to invite me to look him up if I ever chanced to find myself back in Burundi alone."

Thomas guffawed. I'm afraid I probably looked just a tiny bit priggish.

"Are you at least a little jealous?" Sandy teased.

"Keep it up, Mrs. Curry," Thomas said, hugging her tightly. "Just remember that crack about eating my next meal standing up, and think about who has sixty pounds on whom."

It was Sandy's turn to burst into delighted laughter as she rubbed her forehead on his chest.

35

Columbus Day, 1963

Columbus Day is a federal holiday, and the courts as a rule aren't open. Throughout the 1960s, though, one federal court always held a Columbus Day session in order to take care of a single piece of judicial business. Around four-thirty in the afternoon, it was drawing to a close.

". . . I take this oath freely," the judge was saying, tears in his eyes and his voice barely under control. I happened to know that his grandparents had had their last name shortened at Ellis Island and hadn't spoken English the longest day they lived.

"I TAKE THIS OATH FREELY," Sandy and one hundred and eight other people standing with their right arms raised repeated in unison.

". . . without any mental reservation or purpose of evasion."

"WITHOUT ANY MENTAL RESERVATION OR PURPOSE OF EVASION."

194

"Congratulations," the judge said. He'd given his speech before administering the oath. Now there was nothing to do but wrap things up. "You are American citizens."

The clerk's gavel rapped sharply.

"Court will stand adjourned," the clerk barked. "God save the United States of America and this honorable court."

Thomas and I pushed forward through the happy, milling crowd to shake hands with Sandy. Her elegant dove gray dress with a muted crosshatch pattern woven into the collar and bodice, her perfectly coiffed black hair, and the blue eyes shining in her radiant brown face seemed removed by an infinity of time and space from the khaki bush clothes and battle-scarred expression I'd seen on her a little over three months before in Burundi. So did Thomas's understated glen-plaid suit and smooth self-assurance.

But it wasn't as if Burundi had never happened. Burundi had happened. What had happened there had reminded them both of something within themselves that all the trust funds and designer clothes and inspirational rhetoric in the world couldn't conjure away. If Sandy or Thomas had been swinging the fire extinguisher in that helicopter instead of me, it would've been a once-in-a-lifetime experience for the Tutsi pilot. I could tell just by looking at them that it was never going to be as if Burundi hadn't happened.

I'd made reservations at McGonigle's for an early, cele-bratory dinner. I tried to excuse myself early because I thought I saw a private-joke glint in Sandy's eye, and I assumed she'd like to be alone with Thomas to share it with him. Sandy wouldn't hear of it, though, so I ended up waiting through salad, braised lamb chops, roasted potatoes, and baked Alaska for the shoe to drop. It didn't come until after the dessert had been cleared. Thomas waited for Sandy to take out her ciga-rettes, and, after a decent interval had passed without her doing so, he offered her one of his own.

"No, thank you," she said innocently.

Thomas's face paled and feral terror crept into his eyes. He looked as if he were confronting a prospect vastly more horrifying than slugging it out with a squad of Watusi para-troops.

"Sandy," he said with a shaky voice, "please don't tell me you've given up smoking."

"Of course I have not given up smoking—" Sandy said.

"Thank God," Thomas sighed with infinite sincerity.

"—in the sense of abandoning the practice definitively. I have merely stopped smoking for, let me see, the next seven months and two weeks, roughly."

"Seven months and two weeks?" Thomas asked, puzzled. "That's too long for Lent. Is this some Catholic thing you haven't told me about?"

"We have no monopoly whatever on it."

The light dawned.

"You're, ah, you're—" Thomas sputtered.

"*Enceinte,*" I said, helpfully supplying the missing term as I stood up. "Congratulations to both of you and excuse me. This time I am going. Otherwise Thomas'll have to speak French all night."

I waved their *pro forma* protests aside and went to find the *maître d'hôtel* so that I could make sure the dinner bill went on my tab. In 1963, you didn't go around using the word "pregnant" to your wife in the presence of another man.

It's absurd, I know. But a little absurdity isn't all bad. You can take that on faith.